"Tell me the truth, Kat."

He reached out and took her by the shoulders, his piercing green eyes glittering dangerously. "You didn't love me five years ago. You played with me. You found me vastly entertaining, but that's all it ever was for you, right?"

"That's not true." The pain of that day when he'd gotten on a plane and flown out of her life radiated through her now.

Nate snorted derisively and dropped his hands from her shoulders, as if he couldn't stand touching her. "Sure, you loved me so much you weren't willing to sacrifice anything."

"You asked me to be someone I'm not. But I did love *you*. I loved you like I've never loved anyone before…or since."

And she still loved him. But it didn't matter. He hated her and she loved him and the duration of her stay in Boston promised to be sheer heartbreaking torture.

Dear Reader,

I've put together a list of Silhouette Romance New Year's resolutions to help you get off to a great start in 2004!

- Play along with our favorite boss's daughter's mischievous, matchmaking high jinks. In *Rules of Engagement* (#1702) by Carla Cassidy, Emily Winters—aka the love goddess—is hoping to unite a brooding exec and feisty businesswoman. This is the fifth title in Silhouette Romance's exclusive, six-book MARRYING THE BOSS'S DAUGHTER series.

- Enjoy every delightful word of *The Bachelor Boss* (#1703) by the always-popular Julianna Morris. In this modern romantic fairy tale, a prim plain Jane melts the heart of a sexy playboy.

- Join the fun when a cowboy's life is turned inside out by a softhearted beauty and the tiny charge he finds on his doorstep. *Baby, Oh Baby!* (#1704) is the first title in Teresa Southwick's enchanting new three-book miniseries IF WISHES WERE… Stay tuned next month for the next title in this series that features three friends who have their dreams come true in unexpected ways.

- Be sure not to miss *The Baby Chronicles* (#1705) by Lissa Manley. This heartwarming reunion romance is sure to put a satisfied smile on your face.

Have a great New Year!

Mavis C. Allen
Associate Senior Editor

Please address questions and book requests to:
Silhouette Reader Service
U.S.: 3010 Walden Ave., P.O. Box 1325, Buffalo, NY 14269
Canadian: P.O. Box 609, Fort Erie, Ont. L2A 5X3

Rules of Engagement

CARLA CASSIDY

Marrying The Boss's Daughter

SILHOUETTE *Romance*®

Published by Silhouette Books

America's Publisher of Contemporary Romance

Special thanks and acknowledgment are given
to Carla Cassidy for her contribution to the
MARRYING THE BOSS'S DAUGHTER series.

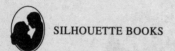 **SILHOUETTE BOOKS**

ISBN 0-373-19702-0

RULES OF ENGAGEMENT

Books by Carla Cassidy

CARLA CASSIDY

is an award-winning author who has written over fifty books for Silhouette. In 1995, she won Best Silhouette Romance from *Romantic Times* for *Anything for Danny*. In 1998, she also won a Career Achievement Award for Best Innovative Series from *Romantic Times*.

FROM THE DESK OF EMILY WINTERS

Two
~~Six~~ Bachelor Executives To Go

Bachelor #1: Love, Your Secret Admirer
Matthew Burke—Hmm...his sweet assistant ~~clearly~~ has googly eyes for her workaholic ~~boss.~~ Maybe I can make some office ~~magic happen.~~

Bachelor #2: Her Pregnant Agenda
Grant Lawson—The guy's a ~~dead~~ ringer for Pierce Brosnan—who ~~wouldn't~~ want to fall into his strong, protective arms!

Bachelor #3: Fill-in Fiancée
Brett Hamilton—The ~~playboy~~ from England is really a British lord! ~~Can I~~ find him a princess...or has he found her already?

Bachelor #4: Santa Brought a ~~Son~~
Reed Connors—The ~~ambitious~~ VP seems to have a heavy heart. ~~Only his~~ true love could have broken it. But where is she now?

Bachelor #5: Rules of Engagement
Nate Leeman—Definitely a lone wolf kind of guy. A bit hard around the edges, but I'll bet there's a tender, aching heart inside.

Bachelor #6: One Bachelor To Go
Jack Devon—The guy is so frustratingly elusive. Arrogant and implacable, too! He's going last on my matchmaking list until I can figure out what kind of woman a mystery man like him prefers....

Chapter One

Nate Leeman stood at his office window and watched as big, fat snowflakes drifted lazily down from an overcast sky. It always surprised him when somebody mentioned how beautiful Boston could be in January.

As far as Nate was concerned, snow meant only one thing…longer commutes to and from the office. Many a wintry night he had camped out at work rather than fight traffic and inclement conditions. Of course most nights he'd just as soon be here as at home.

Here, was his office at Wintersoft, Inc. As Senior Vice President of Technology, he commanded a large office outfitted with a wet bar he'd never used, an ornate armoire containing a television, stereo and

DVD player he'd never touched and a sofa sleeper he'd never unfolded.

All he cared about sat on his enormous desk—his state-of-the-art computer and supporting equipment. The computer and its programs and files weren't just his work; they were his life and, despite all the security precautions, somebody had violated it.

Now his computer wasn't alone on his big desk. A second monitor and keyboard sat next to his and the sight of it only served to heighten the irritation that had been with him since the moment he'd awakened that morning.

A knock sounded on his office door. "Come in," he called and turned away from the window.

Emily Winters, Senior Vice President of Global Sales and the boss's daughter, entered and immediately sat on the burgundy sofa opposite Nate's desk. "The forecast is for two to four inches by midnight."

"What time does her plane arrive?" he asked. Kathryn Sanderson was a private investigator specializing in tech crimes and a part of his past he'd just as soon never encounter again.

Emily looked at her watch. "In an hour."

"Then there shouldn't be any problems," he replied. He hoped his personal feelings about the subject didn't color his words or tone. As far as he was concerned he wouldn't care if bad weather kept Kathryn's plane circling Logan International Airport for days.

He didn't want her here. He didn't need her help.

Unfortunately, he wasn't the boss. Emily's father, Lloyd, was and it had been his and Emily's idea to hire outside help. It had been sheer serendipity that they had chosen a woman—the only woman with whom he'd shared a tumultuous history.

"I've booked her a room at the Brisbain so she'll be close to the office." Emily tucked a strand of her shoulder-length brown hair behind an ear, her blue eyes troubled as she gazed at him.

"We've got to get to the bottom of this, Nate. We've got too much time and too much money tied up in the Utopia program for it to be tampered with and leaked to our competitors."

"Trust me, I'm as upset about this as you are," he replied.

She stood and smoothed the skirt of the sapphire dress that perfectly matched the hue of her eyes. "Father and I are confident that you and Kathryn will be able to get to the source of the security breach. You're two of the best in the business." She headed for the door. "I'll send her in as soon as she arrives so you can put your heads together and find the hack who's creating our problems." With these words she left the office.

Nate sank down at his desk, a frown tugging his features. It wasn't just some hapless hack who had managed to breach the main computer and break into the Utopia program and personnel files. It had been somebody with considerable computer savvy.

From his bottom desk drawer he withdrew two

magazines. Both were computer tech periodicals and each had an article on Kathryn Sanderson…aka Tiger Tech. Born and raised in Silicon Valley, in the past five years Kathryn had made a name for herself in catching computer criminals. She'd not only worked for big business but had also consulted with several police departments as well.

Accompanying one of the articles was a small photo. Although the picture was a little bit fuzzy, it depicted a young woman with a slender face, large eyes and short auburn hair.

The picture didn't do her justice. The way he remembered, her face was slender but always animated with an abundance of confidence, laughter and life. There was no way a photo could capture the exact color of her hazel eyes for they were always changing—sometimes blue, sometimes green, and always sparkling.

And that short auburn hair was shot through with sun-kissed highlights that glistened and shone, adding a multitude of dimension to the color of auburn.

He slammed the magazine shut and stuffed it back into his bottom drawer. He'd told her goodbye five years ago and had assumed he'd never see her again. He didn't want to see her again. She'd been the one risk he'd taken in his life…the one and only gamble he'd been willing to take. He didn't take risks anymore—the outcome was far too painful.

He frowned and rolled his shoulders to release

some of the tension that had taken root in a spot in the center of his shoulder blades.

All he needed was a little more time and he could figure out, on his own, where the breach in the program was coming from.

He punched up his computer, all set to get to work. Maybe he could have the problem solved before Tiger Tech even got off her plane. Then she could just climb on the next flight back to California.

He'd only been working for a minute or two when another knock on his door broke his concentration. "Come in," he said in frustration.

Carmella Lopez, Executive Assistant to Lloyd Winters, entered carrying a fruit basket tied up in pretty cellophane. She smiled, her natural warmth radiating in the depths of her chocolate-brown eyes.

"Mr. Winters thought it would be nice if you'd give this to Ms. Sanderson when she arrives." She set the bountiful basket on the coffee table in front of the sofa.

"How nice," Nate said, trying to ignore the irritation that rose inside him. Maybe he should just roll out a red carpet. Certainly everyone in the entire place seemed eager to make Kat feel welcome. "I'm sure she'll appreciate it."

"We appreciate her coming all the way out here to help us," Carmella replied.

Nate knew he was being rather childish, but he couldn't help it. Utopia was his baby, and Lloyd and Emily Winters were telling him to hand over his baby to the woman who'd once broken his heart. Of course, nobody knew about his former connection to Kat and he didn't intend to share the information with anyone.

Carmella glanced out the window where the snow was falling at a faster rate than last time he'd looked. "They've changed the forecast to four to eight inches by evening. I hope Ms. Sanderson knows how to dress for winter weather."

It was just like Carmella to worry about such a thing. She was always fretting over somebody. She often made Nate rather uncomfortable by straightening his tie or brushing lint off his jacket. He wasn't accustomed to being touched.

Carmella looked out the window once again and muttered something in Spanish beneath her breath. He looked at her quizzically. She smiled. "I said, beautiful but treacherous. And now I'll let you get back to your work."

When she left, Nate stared at the basket of fruit. The staff of Wintersoft, Inc. could welcome Kathryn Sanderson to the fold all they wanted. But they didn't have to work with her, he did.

Beautiful but treacherous. That not only described the snow falling outside the window but could also apply to Kathryn Sanderson.

He walked over to the window and drew a deep breath, steeling himself for the experience of seeing her again.

Emily Winters was waiting for Carmella when she stepped out of Nate's office. She grabbed the attractive Hispanic woman by the arm and pulled her into an empty conference room.

"What's wrong?" Carmella asked.

"I think it's time we stopped our little research plot. With Kathryn and Nate trying to find our hacker, we just can't risk accessing any more personnel files."

"Whatever you think is best," Carmella agreed. "We only have two men left anyway."

"And the odds of Nate Leeman and Jack Devon getting married anytime soon are astronomical," Emily replied. Nate Leeman didn't seem to realize women existed and Jack Devon always had a different model babe on his arm at company functions.

The two women parted and Emily went into her own office and closed the door. She sank down at her desk and thought about the scheme she'd hatched with Carmella five months before.

It had been Carmella who had overheard Emily's father in a phone conversation indicating that he meant to hint to the bachelors in the top positions of his company that it might be a good idea to take an interest in his daughter.

Emily had been appalled, especially since she'd already married a company man and the end result had been a divorce more than four years ago. To counter her father's plans she and Carmella had devised a plot of their own.

It was a crazy plan. Carmella had agreed to research the six bachelors in top company positions and it was Emily's job to find them the perfect match.

So far their plan had worked unbelievably well. Four of the six bachelors had found love, leaving only the loner Nate and the elusive Jack unattached.

But now she had bigger problems than her father's matchmaking. She didn't want anyone to know it had been her and Carmella who had accessed the personnel files in order to marry off the men. She would be humiliated if that information became common knowledge.

It wasn't as if what they had done had been illegal. Certainly it was within Carmella's job description to have access to the personnel files. But, she and Carmella had snooped and, even though everything had turned out well for everyone so far, Emily didn't want to press their luck any further.

However, more important than any humiliation she might suffer was the genuine threat to the company by a hacker who had managed to access some of the Utopia files.

Utopia was the working name for a revolutionary financial software program that Nate had been developing on behalf of Wintersoft, Inc. It had been in the works for months and months and the projected date for completion was fast approaching.

She only hoped Nate and Kathryn Sanderson could find the hacker who threatened to destroy not only months of work but the company's reputation and financial platform.

* * *

Kathryn Sanderson stood on the sidewalk on Milk Street in downtown Boston. Directly in front of her was the fifty-story glass-and-steel building that housed Wintersoft, Inc.

She knew they would be waiting for her arrival, but she wasn't ready to go inside yet. She couldn't believe she was actually in Boston, home of Paul Revere's midnight ride, the Boston Tea Party, baked beans and a little tavern where everyone knew your name.

She tipped her head back and allowed the big, fat snowflakes to tickle her eyelashes, light on her cheeks and melt on her mouth.

Snow was a glorious, wondrous sight and sensation for a woman who'd never been out of California before. The novelty of the weather pumped her full of adrenaline, chasing away the exhaustion left behind by the long plane trip.

She knew it wasn't the snow alone that had created the new burst of nervous energy. It was a combination of the snow and the anticipation of seeing him again.

Nate. It had been over five years since they'd parted. She'd just turned twenty-six when he'd come to Silicon Valley to take some computer courses she was enrolled in as well.

They'd dated for four months before it had all fallen apart and he'd returned to his life in Boston and she'd continued her life in California.

She looked up at the top of the fifty-story building.

She'd been told his office was on the forty-ninth floor. "Senior Vice President of Technology," she murmured aloud.

Apparently he'd achieved his dream of a position of power in the corporate world. She wondered if he'd also attained a corporate wife to go with his position.

No sense in putting it off any longer, she thought. She had a job to do. She shifted her suitcase from one hand to the other, then headed into the office building. She chose the express elevator and was whisked silently and efficiently to the forty-ninth floor.

A secretary who introduced herself as Mary Sharpe greeted her and accompanied her down a long hallway. "That's Nate's office," she said, and pointed to the door at the end of the hallway.

For a long moment Kat stood outside the door, surprised to discover that what she thought might be pangs of hunger were actually nervous butterflies.

It was ridiculous to be nervous about seeing a man she had dated so many years ago. But it had been more than just dating, a little voice whispered inside her head. It had been your future, and you blew it.

She shook her head to quiet the tiny voice. It hadn't been her future. Nate had been a dream, an extended dream that had eventually turned into a nightmare of heartache and false expectations. And now he was the man she would be working with to solve a company problem.

With a deep breath to steady her nerves, she

knocked briskly on the door. She had no preconceptions about the man he'd become in the past five years, but when he opened his office door his appearance sent a small shock wave rippling through her.

It was like stepping back in time. His hair was as rich and black as she remembered. The brilliant green of his eyes was just the same. The gray suit he wore seemed to love the lean fitness of the body it hugged. He hasn't changed a bit, she thought with a small sense of wonder.

"Hi, Nate."

He nodded, his eyes revealing no emotion whatsoever. "Kathryn."

Kathryn. Not Kat, like it had always been, but the more formal Kathryn. "May I come in?"

"Of course." He held the door open wider to allow her to sweep past him. His sensual lips were compressed together in a tight, grim line.

"Wow, nice office," she exclaimed as she stepped in and dropped her suitcase to the floor. She shrugged off her coat and tossed it onto the leather sofa.

It was a beautiful office, the furniture warm in colors of gold and burgundy and rich, highly polished mahogany wood. She stepped to the huge windows and peered out. Through the falling snow, she thought she could see the distant gleam of the harbor.

"I can't believe I'm really in Boston," she murmured.

"I can't believe it, either."

She turned and eyed him sharply. His tone had betrayed a hint of displeasure, but his handsome features held an utter lack of expression.

"The fruit is for you," he said, and indicated the large basket in the center of the coffee table.

"Oh, how lovely. Thank you so much. That was very thoughtful."

"It's not from me," he said hurriedly. "You can thank Mr. Winters."

"Fine, I'll do just that." Kat had been in awkward situations before, but never with the kind of tension that filled the air at the moment.

She sank onto the burgundy sofa and looked up at him. "So, how have you been, Nate? You're looking well." That was the understatement of the century. He looked better than well. He looked fantastic and she was shocked to feel an old familiar spark ignite within her, a spark she mentally doused with cold water.

"I've been fine…good actually…great, in fact." His voice was still cool and he seemed to be looking at everything in the office except her. "The only blight in my life at the moment is the hacker who has been wreaking havoc with my program."

She didn't miss the fact that he'd managed to deflect the conversation from anything personal back to the business at hand. "Then I guess we need to start with some information. When Emily Winters contacted me she was rather vague about the specifics."

"She would have been vague on the phone," he

replied. "The program has been kept under the tightest of security."

"It can't be that tight if somebody got in," she replied wryly.

He was obviously not amused by her observation. He shot her a dirty look and sat down in his chair behind his desk. "I started work on Utopia a little over two years ago. My idea was to come up with a financial program that would streamline cross-functional business processes, eliminate islands of automation and seamlessly integrate enterprise-wide and mission-critical data in real time."

"I thought that was already what Wintersoft, Inc. was offering its clients." She crossed her legs, aware that for the first time his features held an expression other than vague displeasure.

"It was—it is—but Utopia does it all more quickly and efficiently."

As he told her about the features of the beta software program he'd been working on, his features came alive, making him impossibly handsome, making her remember a time when his face had lit up with life just for her. He got up from the desk, pacing as he spoke.

"If time is of the essence, then I guess we should get to work," she said when he'd finished.

There were a million questions she wanted to ask him and none of them had to do with the program he'd been working on. She wanted to know if he still buttered his toast with the precision of a surgeon. She wondered if his favorite color was still blue, if he was still driven by demons she'd never quite understood.

She wanted to know if he had found happiness. If he had a loving wife and maybe a little boy or girl waiting for him at home.

More than anything, she wondered if he ever thought of her and those wonderful, crazy, intense days and nights they had spent together.

She had a feeling the answer was no. She'd always figured that for Nate she had been like a new computer game, and when he realized he couldn't program her he'd closed the file and had never opened it again.

"I just want you to know up front, I'm not accustomed to working with anyone. I'm not used to sharing my space." For the first time since she had arrived, his gaze locked with hers. Emanating from his green eyes was a coolness that blew through her like a wintry wind.

She forced a carefree grin. "Then get used to it, sweetheart, because I'm going to be in your space and in your face until we get this problem solved."

She stood, straightened her sweater and plopped down in the biggest, most comfortable chair at the desk, the one he had just vacated.

Chapter Two

He couldn't stand her. At that moment he couldn't think of what on earth had possessed him years ago to believe himself in love with her.

As she wiggled into his leather chair, he wondered if she'd worn the blue sweater on purpose, if she'd remembered that he'd once told her his favorite color was blue.

The sweater was one of those fuzzy things and looked as if it would be soft to the touch. He also couldn't help but notice that the sweater emphasized the thrust of her full breasts.

The more he thought about it, the more he was sure she'd worn the sweater on purpose, just to irritate him.

"You're in my chair," he said crisply.

"Does it matter? There are two chairs and two computers." She looked up at him innocently.

"Yes, it does matter. I need to be on my own computer. There are things on it I need to work on that you won't be able to access, things that have nothing to do with the Utopia program."

"Oh, okay." She got out of his chair and sat in the one next to his.

Again settled in his own chair, he couldn't help but smell her. It was the same way she'd smelled years ago—a blend like sunshine and citrus, fresh and clean and just a bit tangy.

He remembered watching her one morning as she spritzed herself with the scent, amazed to see her spray the perfume not only in the hollow of her throat and behind her ears, but also behind her knees. She'd explained to him that fragrance always drifts upward, thus the spray behind the knees.

"Are we going to work or are you just going to sit there with a half smile on your face?" she asked.

He slammed back to the present. If there'd been a half smile on his face, it disappeared into a frown of irritation.

He was being punished. He wasn't sure why, or what he had done to spit at the Fates, but they were obviously angry with him. That's why they had sent Kat back into his life.

"We're going to work," he snapped. He opened his top drawer, pulled out a piece of paper and handed it to her.

"You signed all the confidentiality agreements?" he asked.

She nodded. "They've been signed, sealed and delivered."

"This is your password to gain entry into the program. Memorize it and, whatever you do, don't share it with anyone else."

"Oh rats, I had planned to meet some Boston boy babe tonight and whisper my password into his ear."

"I don't find you amusing in the least." He slammed his drawer shut.

"Ah, then I guess it's good that I find myself amusing enough for both of us." The smile on her face disappeared and her eyes narrowed slightly. "Don't talk to me like I'm a bubbleheaded bimbo, Nate. I know the importance of keeping a password secure."

A flush worked itself up his neck. She was right. He'd been condescending. "Sorry," he muttered.

"Your gracious apology is accepted," she replied. She looked at the password, a combination of numbers and symbols, then handed it back to him and turned on the monitor in front of her. "Now, what I need to do is take some time to familiarize myself with the system before I take a look at your program."

He nodded and focused his attention on his own monitor. He could certainly occupy his time while she became acquainted with the particular software they used.

For a few minutes there was silence. If not for the

tantalizing scent of her, he could almost forget she sat next to him.

Almost.

He found himself casting surreptitious glances her way, comparing the way she looked now to the way she had looked five years ago when he'd been so besotted with her. Five years ago they had both been twenty-six years old. She'd changed little in the passing years.

Her hair was still a wavy auburn cap, the short cut emphasizing her high cheekbones and dark-fringed, large hazel eyes. She was tall and slender and his mind flashed with a vision of her in the tiny bright yellow bikini she'd worn when they'd gone to the beach together.

The memory made the room feel overly warm and he could almost smell the tang of salty air mixed with the fragrance of the coconut-oil suntan lotion he'd spread on her back. He could almost feel the slick silk of her skin beneath his fingers, the press of her slender body against his own.

"Hey, you've got Solitaire in here," she said with delight.

"There won't be time for playing games," he replied, grateful for the interruption in his thoughts. The way they'd been headed, he would have needed to take a cold shower within minutes.

"There's always time for Solitaire," she protested. "I do some of my best thinking on other things when I'm playing that game."

It was exactly the reason he'd loaded the game into the computer, because he found that his mind worked out other problems while playing a game of Solitaire.

He wasn't about to admit that to her. The fact that they had anything in common appalled him.

It had been because he'd thought they shared a lot of things five years ago that he'd made a fool of himself. He wasn't about to allow that to happen again.

She pushed back a little from the desk and grabbed her purse. She withdrew a packet of crackers and opened them, gazing at him thoughtfully. "Now, tell me again what makes you suspect a hacker has been accessing the Utopia files."

He couldn't believe she was going to eat at his desk. Apparently his feelings showed on his face.

"Sorry," she said, gesturing to the crackers, "but the food on the plane sucked." She bit into a cracker and he tried not to focus on the crumbs that appeared on the edge of the desk. "What makes you think somebody is hacking into your Utopia program?"

"Everything seemed fine until about a month ago." Nate stared at his computer screen in front of him as he explained the situation. It was still too soon not to find looking at her too much of a distraction to his thought process.

"Then, about a month ago I noticed the first segment of the program showed up as having been copied and a string here and there had been changed, making the whole thing unworkable. I thought maybe one of the techs working with me had made some adjustments for one reason or another.''

He rose from the desk chair and paced the floor in front of the coffee table. ''I fixed the problem area and made a mental note to discuss it with the techs but then forgot about it. Then about a week later I discovered the same thing, only it was in another segment of the program. At that time I spoke to the tech team to see if anyone was trying to make improvements and was carelessly making errors, but none of them admitted to doing it.''

She popped another cracker into her mouth and pulled a bottle of water from her oversize purse. ''How many techs have access to the program?''

''Our five top people, that's it.'' He sat back down and tried not to notice the familiar, delectable scent of her.

''And what do you know about them?''

He frowned. ''What do you mean?''

''What do you know about them? You know, their families, their personal lives? What kind of people are they?''

He looked at her blankly. ''They're very bright and hardworking,'' he began. ''They've been with me since I was hired on.''

''What about their personal lives?'' she pressed. She looked at him in astonishment, obviously seeing the clueless expression on his face. ''You've been working with these people for almost five years and you don't know anything about their personal lives?''

He felt a censure in her words and it irritated him. "I don't have time to socialize. I work with these people, I don't visit with them."

"Why doesn't that surprise me," she muttered under her breath.

"Whatever you're thinking, it's wrong," he replied. "I trust the people I work with implicitly."

"What possible reason could anyone have for copying segments of the program?" She crooked a perfectly formed auburn eyebrow upward.

Had she married? The question popped into his head unbidden. Nothing that he'd read about her indicated she had a spouse, but the articles had focused solely on her work. He quickly checked her left hand, where no ring adorned her finger.

"Nate? Why would somebody be copying the program?" she repeated.

"That's easy, it would have to be to sell. Wintersoft has dozens of competitors who would love to get their hands on this program before its release."

"Of course, a copy of this program would be worth lots of money."

"A small fortune," he agreed. "We've heard through the grapevine that one of our competitors has more information about the Utopia program than they should. I'm thinking someone in their technology department has figured out a way to break into our system."

"Okay, then I guess the best place to start is at the beginning." With the lightest of touches, she pulled up the icon for the Utopia program and typed in the password he'd given her.

"Before I can really start any investigative work, I need to spend some time with the program."

He looked at his watch. "I've got a meeting to attend on another matter. I should be back here in an hour or so." He hesitated, hating the fact that he was leaving her alone in his private sanctum for any length of time and yet desperately needing some space.

"Don't worry, Nate. I won't bounce on your sweet leather sofa or drink all your booze while you're gone. I promise I won't even open one of your desk drawers."

He hoped not. The last thing he wanted was for her to open his bottom drawer, look inside and see the magazines that had the articles on her inside.

"I'll see you when I get back," he said tersely, and left the office.

He'd lied. There was no meeting to attend, no reason for him to have left. Rather, he'd needed to get some air, get the smell of her out of his nose, calm the nerves that she'd seemed to get on from the moment she'd first entered his office.

He stood in the hallway, for a moment unsure where to go. He didn't even know where the employee lounge was. He'd never been there.

Taking the elevator, he went down to the bottom floor of the building and stepped outside, where he hoped a blast of frigid air would freeze out all thoughts of a beach, a blanket and a woman named Kat.

He'd been brilliant five years ago when they'd both gone to the same specialized school in California. She'd been there as a scholarship student and he'd been there under his own financial auspices.

Although she'd immediately been drawn to his brooding, dark good looks, his mind had attracted her as well.

As she worked through the Utopia program files, his brilliance was evident once again. If he was independent, this program would make him a multi-millionaire, as it was she could understand why Wintersoft was worried about a breach in the security of the program.

As she scanned the files, she tried not to notice the subtle scent of expensive cologne that still wafted in the air. It was a different scent than what he'd worn five years before, but certainly just as appealing.

She got up from the desk and grabbed an orange from the fruit basket on the coffee table. After sitting back down at the desk, she peeled the orange and stared at the monitor, her thoughts still filled with the man who had just left the room.

The school they had attended in Silicon Valley had been a six-month term and it had taken her two months to get the bright, handsome Nate away from his computer and into enjoying life.

"Ancient history," she muttered aloud as she finished peeling the orange. As she ate the slices, she marveled at the complexities of what he'd developed and all that was at stake if a hacker was stealing portions of the program.

She lost track of time as she explored the features of Utopia. She had just hit a glitch in the program when Nate returned to the office.

She saw his look of dismay as he took in her orange peels on a napkin in front of her. "Sorry," she said, and scooped the peels into a trash can next to the desk. "Guess you don't munch and work in the same place."

"I never eat or drink at the computer."

"I always eat and drink at the computer," she said. She'd forgotten how rigid he could be, how compulsive in habit. "Did you know you have a glitch?"

He stood behind her and saw where she was at in the program. "Yeah, that's the only problem I have left to solve before it's done."

"It's brilliant, Nate," she said, and enjoyed the first real hint of a smile that crossed his face.

"Thanks." He slid into his chair and his features lit with animation, making him not just handsome but sexy as all get-out. "I've worked it in my head for months, visualized it for years. I still can't believe it's finally coming together."

"All we have to do is catch one little nasty hacker before he messes it up," she said.

The half smile fell from his lips and he nodded. "So far a total of five sections have been copied and subtly changed. I haven't been able to find out how the hacker is entering the system.''

"You must have an open back door somewhere," she said.

"I'm aware of that. I just haven't been able to figure out where it is.''

He'd seemed rather churlish to her before he'd left for his meeting and she'd hoped he'd be in a better frame of mind when he returned, but if anything he seemed more tense.

"I'm sure we'll be able to find the portal and close it up tight,'' she said in an attempt to ease his mind. Her words seemed to have the opposite effect on him.

"If I'd just had a little more time I'm sure I could have figured it out on my own,'' he replied.

Pride. Good grief, she thought. What she was dealing with here was apparently wounded male pride. "I'm sure that's true. But, hopefully with time being of the essence and two of us working to solve the problem, we can do it in half the time.''

"Hopefully, we can solve it in no time at all and you can get back to your life in California.''

She was suddenly tired, and more than a little bit irritated. From the moment she'd stepped into his office, he'd done nothing to make her feel welcome. She'd had a long plane ride, hadn't eaten properly all day and decided at that moment that what she wanted to do was check into her hotel room, get a hot meal and better prepare herself for working side by side with the reluctant Nate.

"There's nothing I'd love better than to solve this problem right now and get out of your hair, but I'm going to get settled in my hotel for the night and start fresh in the morning." She stood and turned off her monitor.

She picked up her coat from the arm of the leather sofa and pulled a key from the pocket as he got up from his chair. "If you could just direct me to the Brisbain Hotel."

"It's two blocks from here. As you exit the building go left and you can't miss it. I'll call you a cab." He picked up the phone.

"No, it's ridiculous to call a cab to take me two blocks. Besides, I'd rather walk. I definitely could use some fresh air. I've noticed it's very stuffy in here." She hoped he got the jab. She pulled on her coat and grabbed the handle on her suitcase. "I suppose you're in at the crack of dawn most mornings?"

"Nine will be fine," he replied. Had she ever really heard his voice radiating with warmth? Or had it always held that cold, sardonic tone?

She opened the office door. "See you tomorrow, Nate." She pulled her wheeled suitcase out into the hallway and breathed a deep sigh.

She was tired, too tired to concentrate on the program with her thoughts focused too intently on Nate. She'd thought she'd see him again and it would be no big deal. She hadn't expected his surliness and she certainly hadn't expected the twinge in her heart.

Pressing the button on the elevator, she promised

herself that this evening she'd resolve her emotions where he was concerned so she could begin tomorrow focused solely on solving the problem, as she'd been hired to do.

She stepped into the elevator and was surprised when Nate slid through the doors to ride down with her. He'd pulled on a midlength gray coat and looked every inch the successful businessman.

"Going home to the little lady?" she asked as the elevator door whooshed closed.

"There is no little lady."

"Ah, going home to the big lady?"

Almost…almost he smiled, but it was only a promising glimmer in his eyes before it was snuffed out by a scowl. "There is no lady at all. I figured I'd better walk you to your hotel. It's late enough you shouldn't be walking the streets alone."

He held out a hand for her suitcase. For a moment stubbornness made her fingers tighten around the handle, but she was tired and the suitcase was heavy, so she relinquished it to him as the elevator doors opened.

"So, you haven't married?" she asked as they stepped out of the elevator.

"No, what about you?"

"Marriage has never been high on my priority list," she replied.

"Yeah, I seem to remember that." There was a touch of bitterness in his voice, the first real indication

to her that the past they'd shared wasn't totally forgotten.

A responding swell of bitterness rose in her. She
swallowed against it, refusing to give it a voice. There
was nothing to be gained in rehashing a past relationship that wasn't meant to be. There was no reason to
bring up old issues that might make the two of them
working together more difficult.

As they stepped into the office building lobby, the
floor-to-ceiling windows ahead revealed a wintry
wonderland. At least three inches of snow had fallen.

"Oh, Nate! Isn't it beautiful?" She hurried ahead
of him and pushed through the double doors and outside. She twirled around on the sidewalk, her arms
raised to the heavens, where the snow was still coming down at a good clip.

After the tension in the office, the stress of the past
couple of hours, she felt like dancing in the street,
reveling in the snow that was as alien to her as Nate's
taciturn nature.

"It's just snow," Nate said.

"My first snow," she exclaimed.

"Really? So, you never drove up to Oregon or anywhere to experience snow skiing or snowmobiling?"

"Never took the time. It's a long drive to the
mountains."

She picked up a handful of the white snow and
packed it into a ball, then eyed Nate with a wicked
gleam.

"Don't even think about it," he warned.

She didn't. She threw it and it splatted into the center of his chest. He stared down at his coat, then back at her in disbelief. Slowly he released his hold on her suitcase, leaned down and grabbed a handful of snow.

"Nate, no." A giggle escaped her. "I'm sorry. I didn't mean to hit you!" As she saw the intent in his eyes, she turned and ran and was hit square in the back with his snowball.

They made their way toward the Brisbain Hotel one snowball at a time and, more than once, she heard Nate's deep laughter ring out.

She was pleased to know he still had the capacity to laugh. While they had been in his office she'd begun to think he was anatomically incapable of laughter.

She felt warmer than she had since the moment she'd stepped off the plane, despite the frigid temperatures and falling snow.

They stopped in front of the hotel and he reached out to brush the snow off her hair and face. He'd touched her only a moment when all laughter faded from his eyes and he stepped back from her, tension once again radiating from every pore of his body.

"Here you are, safe and sound." He held out her suitcase and she took it from him.

"Thank you for walking me here," she said. "It was quite chivalrous of you."

"Lloyd and Emily Winters would never forgive me

if anything happened to you before the hacker is caught.''

Kat suddenly felt the chill of the air not only around her, but blowing through her as well. For just a moment, as Nate's laughter had filled the air, she'd almost forgotten he was the man who had broken her heart.

She'd almost forgotten he was the man without a heart, the man for whom life held no meaning outside of his work.

"Thanks, anyway," she replied. "I'll see you in the morning."

With a curt nod, he turned on his heels and left, a gray-clad solitary figure against the pristine snow.

She watched until he disappeared from her sight, then she turned and went into the hotel lobby. Wintersoft, Inc. had spared no expense on her room.

The first thing she did when she entered the luxury suite was order in room service. Only when a decent meal was in the works did she unpack her suitcase and change into an oversize T-shirt that served as her sleeping attire.

She hadn't really considered that working with Nate would be so difficult. She hadn't believed that just by looking at him she'd remember the fact that he had been a breathtaking, passionate lover.

But she couldn't forget that those four months she'd spent with him, months of laughing and loving, of craziness and embracing life had been nothing more than a temporary illusion.

It had been four months that Nate had been able to pretend to be human. He'd managed to make her believe he understood people, that he understood her. Her time with him had culminated in the discovery that he was nothing like the kind of man she'd thought him to be.

"Fool me once, shame on you. Fool me twice, shame on me," she said aloud as she stretched out on the sofa with her room service table in front of her.

She'd been fooled by Nate Leeman once in her life. She'd thought that if you cut him, he'd bleed blood like normal people, but she had learned that if you cut him, he bled gigabytes and stuffy Bostonian ideals of home, hearth and wife. She hadn't fit then, and likely never would.

Chapter Three

Nate walked briskly back to the office building, bending slightly into the wind that blew against his face. The only traffic on the street was a city snow truck slowly making its way with a plow lowered against the snowy pavement.

He had no intention of attempting the drive home with the snow still coming down at such a fast pace. The traffic would be horrible now, even worse for the morning commute if the snow continued to fall through the night.

As he walked, he tried to get a mental vision of Kat out of his mind—the vision of her cheeks all pink from the cold, her laughter pealing in the air with abandon, her eyes sparkling with mischief as she formed one snowball after another.

On the journey from the office to the hotel, she'd

danced in the snow, fallen down and made a snow angel and had tried to talk him into building a snowman.

He'd loosened up only enough to lob snowballs at her as she squealed and ran ahead of him. Watching her, so full of life, so completely unaffected by what anyone else might think about her childish play, had stirred something inside him…something distinctly uncomfortable.

He brushed the snow off his coat and stamped his feet as he reentered the lobby of his office building. That was her problem—she had too much spontaneity.

She got an impulse and didn't think, she just acted on it. Her exuberance for life was both infectious and irritating.

He'd always lived in Boston and had never had a snowball fight in his life. Within mere hours of being with Kat, she had him throwing snowballs and acting like a damned childish fool.

"Beautiful but treacherous," he muttered as he hung his coat in the closet and returned to his desk chair.

How she had fooled him in those four months they'd shared a relationship. For the first time in his life he'd realized there was more to life than just computer chips and programs, a life other than diligent study and hard work.

She'd opened up a whole new world to him, a

world where play and leisure were necessary, even demanded if he wanted to spend any time with her.

She'd introduced him to long barefoot walks on the beach, to sleeping late on Saturday mornings. She'd taught him how to play Monopoly and strip poker.

They had explored San Jose street by street, eating in charming little restaurants and shopping in funky stores that sold items he'd never consider wearing.

Nights they usually wound up at the apartment he was renting for the six months of his schooling. She shared a beach house in Santa Cruz with half a dozen young men and women. It was a place that afforded them little privacy and Nate had wanted privacy with her.

She'd made him believe she wanted all the things he did. She'd made him think they were of one mind and spirit when it came to life and love and the future.

When Wintersoft, Inc. had offered him this job, he'd thought it was a perfect beginning for his life with Kat. A great job in his hometown and a lovely wife who would be at his side. Oh yes, he'd been all kinds of fool over her.

He brushed errant cracker crumbs from his desktop into his palm, threw them into the wastebasket, then turned on his computer, consciously attempting to shove thoughts of Kat from his mind.

It was still relatively early, just a little after seven. Maybe if he got back to work he could figure out where the hacker was getting in and where he was coming from before morning.

Then Kat could get back on a plane and take her sparkling hazel eyes, her tantalizing scent and her rich, sexy laughter with her.

A knock on his door pulled him from his thoughts. Emily Winters stepped into the office. "I figured you'd be working late," she said, and looked around the room. "Kathryn isn't here?"

"I just got back from taking her to her hotel. She wanted to get settled in. We'll hit it hard tomorrow," he explained as he stood.

"That's fine. I was hoping to stop by earlier and introduce myself to her, but I've been in meetings until now." She leaned against the door frame. "Now that you've met her, I'm hoping you two will work together well."

"Actually, I knew Kathryn already."

Emily raised an eyebrow in surprise. "You did?"

"We went to tech school together five years ago in California."

"Really?" Her blue eyes held his intently and he wondered if she could see in his eyes that he knew Kat well...very well.

He knew that she gave the best back rubs in the world, remembered the soft gasps she emitted when he caressed her inner thighs, knew that she could surf the ocean waves almost as efficiently as she could surf the Internet.

"She certainly has made a name for herself in the computer industry," Emily continued. "There have

been all sorts of articles about her in several magazines.''

"She doesn't exactly shy away from publicity,"
Nate said dryly.

"From what I've read, she usually works out of
her California office. We were lucky we could talk
her into coming out here. Hopefully, she's just the
person we need. All that's important is that she help
you get to the source of the problem," Emily said.
"Well, I'm getting out of here. If you're driving home
you'd better get started. I've heard the roads are pretty
horrible."

"Okay, thanks." The moment she left his office he
sank back into his chair. It was more than wounded
pride that made him irritated that they'd brought her
in.

It was the fact that he was supposed to be one of
the best in the industry, that somehow he felt he
wasn't living up to his potential.

"A man is only as good as the work he does, the
things he accomplishes." How many times had Nate
heard his mother and father say those very words?
How good could he be if his company had to bring
in outside help?

Thinking of his parents reminded him that he
hadn't spoken to them in almost a month. He made
a mental note to call them in the next day or two.
They rarely called him. They were busy people with
busy lives.

What he needed to do at the moment was go back

into his program and find the hacker, solve the problem and get Kathryn Sanderson forever out of his life.

She slept like a baby, but then she always did. It
seemed no matter what turmoil took place in her daily
life, it left her alone the moment she closed her eyes
for sleep.

She knew she was lucky that way, but had long
ago realized it was some sort of nice compensation
for having to deal with her mother.

As she was growing up, God knows she had needed
every ounce of energy to deal with the daily struggles
of being her mother's daughter, and so had gifted her
with the capacity to sleep well each and every night
and awaken well rested.

She tumbled out of the bed and rushed to the windows to pull open the curtains. She gasped at the sight
that greeted her. Milk Street looked more like Frosty
the Snowman land.

There appeared to be nearly a foot of snow on the
ground and the sun peeking up over the horizon gave
the entire landscape a candy-cane-pink kind of glow.
She admired the beauty of the scene for a moment
then turned away from the window.

The challenges that lay ahead energized her, both
the work involved and Nate Leeman himself.

She felt strong this morning, more than capable of
taking whatever acrimony he decided to dish out. She
knew he could be impossibly closed off from others,
as emotional as a rock and downright surly when he

wanted to be, but she refused to let him get under her skin.

By seven she'd eaten a Danish and drunk two cups of coffee, showered and dressed and decided that spending another minute in the hotel room was impossible.

She grabbed her coat and left. There was nothing to say she couldn't get to work early. Nate had said nine, but if she knew him he'd be in early as well.

As she trudged through the snow the two blocks to the office building, she thought about the fact that he hadn't married. The fact that he was still single certainly didn't surprise her. It would take a very patient, Milquetoast kind of woman to fit into the ideal he had for his wife.

Five years ago she'd had neither the patience nor the fortitude to become the woman he wanted. Nothing had changed, not that he was asking.

She was greeted by the security guard, who had her sign in, then she stepped into the elevator that would whisk her up to the floor that held Nate's office.

The hallway held the hush of early morning. No phones rang, no scurrying footsteps abounded, just the stillness of a building holding its breath in anticipation of the day's beginning.

She was unsurprised to find Nate's office door unlocked. She eased it open, stepped inside, then went completely still.

Nate was there at his desk. It was apparent from the clothes he wore that he'd been there all night. It was also obvious that he was sound asleep slumped over the keyboard, his face turned in her direction.

At some point or another over the course of the night, he'd taken off his suit jacket. His white shirt stretched across the width of his shoulders.

She knew she should awaken him immediately, but she didn't. Instead she studied him in his unguarded, unconscious state.

He was still one of the most handsome men she'd ever known. His features were sharply defined, sculpted by an artist's hands…aristocratic yet utterly masculine.

His dark eyelashes were sinfully long and shadowed the skin just beneath his eyes. His jaw was darkened slightly with the faint growth of a five-o'clock shadow.

His mouth was slightly agape, although no hint of a snore emitted from him. She remembered that mouth on hers, hot and demanding. He may have been unemotional in most aspects of his life, but when it came to his work and lovemaking, he'd been quite passionate.

One minute his eyes were closed and the next minute they were open, vivid green staring at her as if she were an apparition from his dreams.

He jerked up, groaned and instantly rolled his shoulders as if in pain. "What time is it?" he asked, his voice husky and deeper than usual.

"Almost seven-thirty."

"I thought I told you nine."

She shrugged out of her coat and stepped up behind him. "I decided to come early." Before he could rise from the desk, she placed her hands on his shoulders. "Got a kink?"

He started to get up, but then sank back down. "About a million of them," he admitted, then moaned again as her fingers kneaded into his shoulder.

She could feel the taut muscles beneath her fingertips and worked them as he rolled his head forward.

"You were always a sucker for a back or shoulder rub," she said, trying not to enjoy the feel of his muscles beneath the cotton shirt.

"You should have been a professional," he murmured.

She laughed. "Wait until you get my bill." She sobered, deciding it was time to discuss something more difficult. "Nate, I know you aren't particularly happy to have me here."

She instantly felt the tension rip through his muscles once again. "I'm not particularly pleased that Wintersoft had to bring anyone in on this," he replied.

"Somebody else wouldn't have brought any history with her," Kat said. "I just don't want our history to get in the way of us working together companionably. I don't want any hard feelings complicating things."

"Our history is ancient. I certainly don't harbor any

hard feelings toward you. What's past is past." His voice was emotionless.

She wished she could see his face, study his features to see if what he said was true, but the only way she could tell how the conversation was affecting him was by the rigidity of his shoulder muscles beneath her fingers.

"Look, Kat. I know I've been tense, but I've got a lot riding on this program and now some hacker is threatening to screw it all up."

"Relax, Nate. We'll get the hacker," she assured him, hoping, indeed, they could catch the creep messing around with a million-dollar beta software program.

She massaged his shoulders for another few minutes, until she felt the tension leaving, then without her volition, her fingers moved up into the rich, thick dark hair at the nape of his neck.

He jumped up so quickly he nearly knocked her backward. "You can go ahead and get settled in. I'm going to freshen up."

He strode quickly toward the door that she knew led to a luxury bathroom and disappeared inside. Kat's fingers still tingled with the feel of his crisp hair, and her head was suddenly filled with memories of tangling her hand in his hair as they had made love.

She sat in the chair next to his and tried to shove those memories out of her head. Although she'd had other lovers before and since Nate, not many and none as memorable.

There had been something magical between her and Nate, something inexplicable and unforgettable. It had taken her nearly two months to get him to loosen up, open up to her, but the wait had paid off.

During the days in class, they had been fiercely competitive, but the moment class was finished, they'd put that behind them and had spent every spare moment together fiercely and passionately in love.

"In love." She snorted derisively. They hadn't been in love. They'd been in lust, and in a deep denial of the intrinsic difference of their life dreams and vision of their future.

She punched up her computer and stared at the screen as the sound of water running came from behind the closed bathroom door. Executive bathroom, must have a shower, she thought.

Typing in her password to access the Utopia files, she tried not to visualize Nate in the shower. All too easily she remembered exactly what he looked like in a shower, exactly how the water would trace paths through his dark chest hair.

She'd just begun to scan the files when the office door opened and a pretty, dark-haired woman poked her head in. "Ah, I see we have a new early riser. You must be Kathryn." She stepped into the office, a warm smile on her face as Kat stood. She held out a hand to Kat. "I'm Emily Winters."

"Ms. Winters, it's so nice to meet you," Kat replied as they shook hands.

"Please, make it Emily." She gestured Kat back

into the chair. "I'm sorry I didn't get a chance to stop in and introduce myself yesterday, but I was in meetings most of the afternoon. I trust you got settled in all right at the Brisbain?"

"My room is beautiful, thank you, and, please, call me Kat."

"Kat it is." She cocked her head toward the bathroom door. "I'm assuming Nate is in there?"

Kat nodded. "He's freshening up. He spent the night here last night."

"That's no big surprise. I keep telling him I don't know why he keeps paying rent on his condo when he spends almost all his waking and sleeping hours here."

"He was just like that when I first met him. A good work ethic is commendable, but I kept trying to convince him that all work and no play makes a dull Nate."

"I hear Kat is extolling my virtues."

Kat whirled around to see Nate step out of the bathroom. He was perfectly groomed in a three-piece gray suit, crisp white shirt and subdued black-and-gray tie.

He stepped closer, bringing with him the scent of fresh minty soap and a hint of shaving cream and toothpaste.

Emily laughed, an obvious attempt to dispel the tension that snapped in the air. "She isn't exactly spilling state secrets, Nate. Everyone knows that about you. I mean, not that you're dull," she hurriedly continued, "but, that you're a bit of a workaholic."

She turned back to Kat. "Again, it's nice to have you here. Please let me know if there's anything my father or I can do during your stay here in Boston."

"Thanks, I appreciate it."

"We'd better get to work," Nate said the moment Emily had left the office. He sat down at his computer and tapped in his access code.

"You're mad, aren't you?" Kat asked as she slid into her chair.

"Why should I be mad?" He eyed her darkly, his voice as cool as the wind outside.

"Because I told your boss that you're dull."

"Why should that make me mad? You don't know me, Kathryn. It's been five years since we had anything to do with each other. You don't know anything at all about my life." With each word, he sounded more and more defensive.

"You're right," she agreed. However, in the brief time she'd been in Boston, she'd already gleaned enough clues about him to recognize he'd long ago reverted to the isolated, workaholic loner he'd been when she'd first met him. A wave of sadness swept through her, which she quickly shoved aside.

"Tell me now," she said.

He frowned. "Tell you what?"

"Tell me about your life, about your hobbies and your friends."

"My life is really none of your business. Besides

we don't have time for social chatter. We've got work to do.'' With those words he focused on his monitor and she knew he'd tuned her out as effectively as if he'd pushed her power button and turned her off.

One step forward, two steps back, she thought. She'd hoped the brief conversation about their past would dispel all the subtle stress that had been between them. Instead, he seemed as uptight as ever as they began to work.

A back door, a portal—that's what they were looking for, Kat reminded herself as she stared at her own monitor. The hacker had to be slipping through the built-in security measures somehow and, before they could catch him or stop him, they had to figure out how he was getting into the program in the first place.

As they worked silently side by side, reading and rereading, analyzing and dissecting segment by segment of the program files, she wished she could tune out his presence as easily as he'd apparently dismissed hers.

He smelled so good, so fresh and clean, and she found concentrating difficult for the first time in her life. Surreptitiously she found her focus drifting from her keyboard over to his, where his hands occasionally tapped the keys to take him to a new area of the program files.

She'd always liked his hands. For a man who worked the small keys of a computer keyboard, he had relatively big hands.

With a sigh of irritation, she returned to work and

tried not to remember how those hands had felt caressing her back, sliding along her rib cage, raking through her short hair.

Lunchtime came and went and he didn't mention breaking to eat. A competitiveness she'd forgotten she possessed reawakened inside her.

She'd be darned if she'd be the one to insist on a break. She could work just as long and quietly as he could. Besides, once she settled into working, the hours passed quickly and she once again found herself filled with admiration for what Nate had accomplished.

Intelligence in a man had always been attractive to her and Nate's intelligence had come in a package she'd found positively irresistible. Even now, working so close to him, smelling his scent, feeling the heat from his body, stirred her hormones in a way no man had done for a very long time.

Still she had no intention of restarting any kind of a relationship with him, even if he acted as if he was remotely interested in going back to those days and nights they'd spent together.

Saying goodbye to Nate Leeman had been the single most painful thing she'd ever done in her life. She would never again put herself in a position where she had to go through that kind of emotional pain.

Several times through the course of the day Nate was interrupted with phone calls, obviously business calls, and twice he was called away from his office for meetings.

The second time he was gone, Kat pulled a packet of crackers from her purse and grabbed a banana from the basket that still sat in the center of the coffee table.

Thank goodness Lloyd and Emily had decided to send her a basket of fruit and not a floral arrangement. If it had been flowers, she'd probably be munching on crackers and ivy.

She'd just finished her banana and crackers when he returned and slid back into his chair. He frowned at the crumbs on the top of the desk.

"Why must you eat crackers when you work?" he asked as he brushed them off into the palm of his hand and threw them into the trash.

"Because you don't break to eat. We haven't had lunch. It's almost six and you haven't mentioned supper. You might be able to function without food, but I need it to think."

Her voice was sharper than she'd intended, but his stoic silence throughout the day and her still empty stomach made her cranky.

He eyed her in surprise. "If you wanted to stop and eat, why didn't you say so?"

"Because I decided if you could work through meals, then so could I. Because I know how important this is to you and I thought maybe if we worked long enough we'd find the problem. But we aren't any closer now than we were when we started this morning and I'm starving." She expelled a breath of frustration.

"You always did get crabby when you weren't fed properly," he mused.

"If you think this is crabby, wait another hour," she warned. "I'm going to be positively rabid."

"I suppose I could order in a pizza, but only if you promise you won't eat it at my desk."

"At this moment I'd promise to eat it hanging out the window if you'll just place the order."

A small smile curved his lips and the simple, unexpected gesture sent a shaft of sweet heat rushing through her. "I don't think that will be necessary. Pepperoni and mushroom, right?"

It surprised her that he remembered. She nodded. That smile had thrown her for a loop. She'd thought herself inured to any hint of charm Nate might display. But that smile of his. Even after all this time, it still managed to create a feeling of magic inside her.

Hopefully, it was just hunger for a pepperoni and mushroom pizza.

Emily Winters flew out of the last meeting she had scheduled, eager to call it a day and head home. She nearly bumped headlong into a sturdy well-built chest.

"Todd!" She stepped back and frowned at the man who had been her husband what seemed like a million years ago. Actually, they had divorced almost five years earlier, after an eighteen-month disastrous marriage.

"Hi, Emily. Working late as usual?"

Todd Baxter was a handsome man. His blond hair was beginning to recede a bit, but he had an easy, confident smile and pale blue eyes that Emily had learned hid a will of steel.

She'd married him for a combination of reasons—to please her father, because she'd thought they'd make a good match, because he loved Wintersoft as much as she did. She'd thought marriage the next logical step in her life and Todd had been a relentless suitor.

The reasons she'd married Todd had been the wrong reasons and, although the divorce had been painful, remaining with him would have been far more painful.

"I was just on my way home." She eyed him curiously. "What are you doing here at this time of the evening?"

"I'm having drinks with your father."

"Oh." It made her slightly uncomfortable that her father and her ex-husband still maintained a relationship, one that seemed to be getting stronger rather than waning. "I think lately you see more of Dad than I do."

"I enjoy his company and he gives me good advice."

"How's the job search coming?" She knew he'd recently lost his position at another software company when they had done some major downsizing.

"All right. I've got some good prospects. Worldwide was generous with their severance package, so

I'm not desperate to get back to work. In fact, I'm enjoying my time off.''

He surprised her by leaning forward and brushing a strand of her hair back from her shoulder. To her, it felt like an intensely intimate touch, which was no longer his right. She took a step backward, ill at ease.

"You look good, Emily." He gestured toward her suit. "Blue has always been your color. I love seeing you in blue. Well, better get moving, don't want to keep Lloyd waiting." With a jaunty smile, he hurried past her down the hallway.

She smoothed a hand down her skirt, trying to remember the last time Todd had given her any kind of compliment. It felt odd, to receive one from him now.

He'd been a frequent visitor to Wintersoft in the past month or two, a situation that didn't exactly thrill Emily.

Todd had been a rising star in Global Sales at Wintersoft when he and Emily had gotten married. She'd married Todd right out of college, believing it was the logical sequence of life. Besides, Lloyd Winters loved Todd as the son he'd never had and was thrilled when he and Emily married.

She'd believed things would continue as they had after the marriage. They'd both still work at Wintersoft building the company that was her father's dream and her legacy, and the only difference would be after the marriage they'd go home together after work.

She smiled as she saw Carmella coming down the hallway toward her. Her encounter with Todd had thrown her off slightly, so the sight of Carmella's familiar warm smile was welcome.

"I see marathon man is back again."

Emily laughed. Todd was a runner and ran the Boston Marathon every year. "I guess he's having drinks with Dad this evening."

"The best thing you ever did was leave that man. I never did care much for him," Carmella said. "I've never understood your father's fondness for him."

"At the time of our divorce, I was afraid my relationship with Dad was destroyed forever." A flutter of pain swept through her as she remembered the strain the divorce had put on her relationship with her father.

"He was just disappointed, that's all. He thought a lot of Todd and had hoped the two of you would be happy," Carmella said.

Emily nodded. "That's what I'd hoped, too. The minute we said our vows, though, Todd changed all the rules." Todd had made it clear following the ceremony that he was the boss and saw himself taking over the company when Lloyd retired.

Emily's role would be as the wife of a wealthy businessman. He expected her to become a socialite and attend charity functions and events. She hadn't been ready to give up her work at Wintersoft, wasn't sure she'd ever want to retire from this company that was so dear to her heart.

After the divorce Todd had left the company, explaining that it was simply too uncomfortable to be working for her and her father.

She thought of the way Todd had touched her hair, the spark in his eyes as he'd told her he'd always loved seeing her in blue. "I hope Dad isn't trying to push for some sort of a reconciliation between me and Todd."

"I can't imagine such a thing," Carmella replied. "Besides, remember that what I overheard your father telling your aunt was that most of the senior vice presidents are good, acceptable son-in-law material. He didn't mention anything about Todd. Why? Did Todd say something?"

"No, nothing like that." Maybe she was just tired, Emily thought, and seeing things that aren't there. Surely Todd knew better than to think they could ever reconcile. She wasn't even remotely attracted to him anymore.

"How are things going with the new computer guru?" Carmella asked.

"Kathryn seems quite nice, although I sensed some tension between her and Nate."

Carmella nodded, as if unsurprised. "I would assume Nate isn't the easiest man in the world to work with."

Emily smiled as she thought of the pretty auburn-haired woman she'd met that morning. She had a bright sparkle in her eyes, a confident tilt to her head and a self-assured handshake. "I have a feeling Kathryn Sanderson can handle anything Nate can dish out.''

''Well, don't you worry your head about Todd and your father.'' Carmella frowned. ''Have you decided if we need to tell Nate and Ms. Sanderson about me accessing the personnel files?''

''I don't think we should say anything about it yet. It's possible the subject won't come up and, besides, you didn't do anything illegal or wrong.''

Carmella grinned, looking surprisingly impish. ''No, it was just a little bit sneaky.'' Emily must have looked miserable, because Carmella hurriedly continued, ''It was my idea to check out the backgrounds of the eligible bachelors and get them suitable mates before your father could shove them in your direction. If anything comes out about it, I'll take full responsibility.''

Emily reached over and grabbed Carmella's hand. ''If anyone finds out about the plot to marry off all the eligible vice presidents in the company, then we're in it together.'' Emily squeezed Carmella's hand, then released it. ''And now, I'm getting out of here. I have a date with a steaming bath and a cup of hot cocoa.''

Minutes later, as she left the building, she thought of their plan to matchmake for the bachelors she feared her father would try to foist on her.

Up to this point in time their plan had worked beyond their wildest imaginations. Initially, Emily had entertained a million second thoughts about the whole thing, then Carmella had told her that she thought Sarah Morris, assistant secretary to Matt Burke, Senior Vice President of Accounting, was in love with her boss. It had taken a little intervention from Carmella and Emily, but within a month, the two had become engaged.

The second couple Emily hadn't been trying to make a love match, but one had been made nevertheless. Emily had simply been trying to help a very pregnant Public Relations manager named Ariana Fitzpatrick when she'd introduced her to Grant Lawson, the company's General Counsel. She'd hoped Grant would be able to help Ariana deal with the responsibilities her ex-fiancé would owe her upon the birth of the twins she carried.

Grant had offered her not only legal advice, but his hand in marriage as well. In working together on Ariana's problems, she and Grant had fallen in love and their wedding was only weeks away.

Flush with success, Emily and Carmella had moved to the next eligible bachelor on their list—Brett Hamilton, Senior Vice President of Overseas Division. She'd discovered he'd needed a pretend fiancée to stop his English family from arranging a marriage for him. Sunny Robbins, a paralegal in the company, agreed to pose as Brett's pretend fiancée. Carmella and Emily had been delighted when pretend had become real and the two had fallen in love.

The fourth couple had been a pleasure to bring together, a truly romantic story of two people who had lost touch with each other but had rediscovered their love. Reed Connors, the Vice President of Global Marketing had told Carmella that Samantha Wilson in his home town of Fernville, Virginia, had broken his heart years ago.

Carmella did a little checking and found out that Samantha Wilson was a single mom of a little boy…a boy who was the spitting image of Reed. She convinced Reed to attend a wedding in his hometown and it didn't take long for him and Samantha to find each other and their love for each other once again.

Despite her second thoughts about it all, she took a moment to bask in the warmth of knowing she'd been a little bit responsible for eight people finding love and happiness.

Unfortunately, all too quickly her thoughts turned back to her ex-husband.

There had been something almost flirtatious about him today and as much as she tried to convince herself she'd only imagined it, she didn't think she had.

What was he up to? She hoped he wasn't subtly encouraging Emily's father to think that reconciliation between the two of them was possible. The divorce had nearly broken her father's heart and it had taken Emily months to feel as if she'd gotten her relationship with her father back on track. She didn't want to go through anything like that again, but there was no way she would ever entertain thoughts of being Todd Baxter's wife again—or any man's for a long time to come.

Chapter Four

The ringing of the cell phone jarred Nate from his focus on his computer screen. He watched as Kat scrabbled in her purse for the instrument that rang to the tune of "Three Blind Mice."

She'd only received a couple of calls during the week they'd been working together. She'd kept the calls brief and he could tell from her end of the conversation that they'd been from friends back in California.

"Mom!" she said as she answered this call. She got up from the desk and moved toward the windows. "How are you?"

He breathed a small sigh of relief as she walked away from him. The past week had been the most stressful he'd ever endured.

Not only were they getting nowhere in trying to

find where the hacker was entering the program, she was driving him completely and utterly crazy.

Hour after hour he sat next to her, smelling her scent, feeling her heat, listening to the little sounds of frustration that occasionally she emitted.

She did nothing overtly to irritate him, but she irritated him. He told himself it was because he just wasn't accustomed to having somebody in his office when he worked, but it was more than that. It was the memories, the damned memories, that refused to leave him alone.

"That's good, Mom, that's great." Kat's voice intruded, breaking any concentration he'd been trying to attain. He changed positions in his chair, moving just enough so he could see her as she paced in front of the office windows.

Today she was wearing a pair of navy slacks and a white-and-navy long-sleeved blouse. The blouse was tailored and emphasized her slender waist and full breasts.

The sun streaking in the window sparked the red highlights of her auburn hair. Button-size navy earrings adorned her ears. She looked beautiful.

It had been on the second day of them working together, when she'd worn tiny gold hoops at her ears, that he'd remembered how wild she'd been when he'd kissed her earlobes. Were those dainty little earlobes still hot zones for her? He forced his attention back to his monitor.

"No...no, I'm still at work. I know it's late, Mom.

We've been working long hours. No, I haven't seen any of Boston. I know I've been here a week. Yes…yes, I will. I love you, too. Talk to you soon.''

She clicked off and returned to her chair next to his. He tried to remember what she'd told him about her mother when they'd dated for those four glorious months so long ago. At that time, he thought he remembered her telling him that her mother lived in Florida.

''Is your mother still in Florida?'' he asked.

''Florida?'' She looked at him blankly for a moment, then a slight flush colored her cheeks. ''Oh, no. She's been back in California for the past five years. She has an apartment not far from my place.''

''You visit with each other often?''

''Yes, at least every other day or so, although she keeps herself pretty busy.''

''What about your father? I don't remember you ever mentioning him.''

She frowned, the gesture drawing her delicate eyebrows closer together. ''There isn't much to mention. When I was eight, he left my mother for another woman. He stayed in touch with me off and on for about a year, then I never heard from him again.''

Funny, that in those four months they had dated, she'd never told him this. In fact, now that he thought about it, they hadn't talked about much of anything important in those days. They had been too busy laughing and loving, exploring the sights and each other.

He stared at his monitor. Maybe if they'd done more talking, they would have realized quickly how wrong they were for each other. Maybe, if they had discussed some of the important things in life, she wouldn't have ripped his heart out.

He looked at his watch. It was nearly seven. Time to order in something for dinner, as had become the habit the past week.

"What will it be? Pizza?" He turned to look at her once again.

A mutinous expression swept over her features. "No, I don't want pizza."

"Chinese? I know a good take-out service. Their delivery time is fairly quick."

Her frown deepened and the expression of mutiny became one of aggravation. "No. I don't want to order in pizza. I don't want to eat Chinese from paper cartons." She grabbed her mouse and tapped it, closing first one application then another.

"What are you doing?" he asked.

"I'm quitting for the night." The words were clipped, brusque.

"What's wrong?" he asked, wondering what had made her appear mad.

"What's wrong?" She clicked her mouse button one last time and her monitor went dark. "I'll tell you what's wrong. I've been in this city for a little over a week and haven't seen anything except the inside of this office building."

She got out of her chair, as if driven to stand

through sheer adrenaline. "You've worked me like a mule, occasionally dangling take-out food as a carrot in front of my face. I'm not a mule. I'm a person and, unlike you, I'm accustomed to having a life outside of my work."

She stalked over to the closet and grabbed her coat from inside. "I'm going to go out and find a restaurant, where a real person will serve me and I can hear other people talking. I'm going to breathe some fresh air and maybe have a sinfully rich dessert and unwind."

"Wait a minute."

She yanked on her coat and faced him once again. "Wait for what?"

"For me," he replied. He tapped his own mouse and quickly shut down the computer.

Her little spiel had made him feel guilty. She was a stranger to his town just as he'd been a stranger to her town years ago. At that time she'd gone out of her way to show him the beauty of the California city and he had done nothing in the past week to return the favor, except to work her half to death.

He stood, and her face radiated an expression of stunned surprise. "What?"

"I said to wait for me." He walked past her to the closet and grabbed his coat. "You're right. I've been working you like a mule. The least I can do is take you to dinner."

"That isn't necessary," she said stiffly.

"Oh, but I insist. Besides, you don't know the city

so I'm sure you don't know what restaurants are good and which ones aren't so good." He pulled on his coat.

She eyed him suspiciously. "You're going to take me out to dinner at a good restaurant? Is this some kind of a joke? Do you even know what restaurants are good around here?"

He was already regretting the impulse that had prompted his plan of action. Her words did nothing to alleviate his regret. "Of course I know what restaurants are good. I've lived in Boston all my life," he said with an edge of exasperation.

"You may have been in Boston all your life, but that doesn't mean you live in Boston," she muttered.

"And what is that supposed to mean?" They left the office together and headed for the elevator.

"I mean you can be in a city all your life and not really know about it." The elevator arrived and they stepped inside. "I met a guy once who'd lived his whole life in New York City, but he'd never seen the Statue of Liberty, had never seen a Broadway play or ridden the subway. Of course, he was a computer nerd, too."

"Well, that isn't like me. I know Boston inside and out, have visited all the tourist attractions, the museums and historical sights." He wondered if the man from New York had been her lover, not that he cared in the least. "And what do you mean by 'he was a computer nerd, too'? Is that what you think I am?"

The elevator opened and they left the lobby of the building.

"Of course, you're a computer nerd," she replied, then laughed. "Don't look so offended. I'm a computer nerd, too."

He stepped off the curb and hailed a cab. He'd never considered himself a computer nerd before. He'd always just thought of himself as a businessman trying to make his mark in the world of computer programming.

Their conversation halted as a cab pulled up to the curb and they got into the back seat. "The Boston Beanery," he told the driver. He leaned back in the seat. "So, is being a computer nerd a good thing or a bad thing?"

"It can be good or bad. I've met some computer geeks who get so caught up in their computer world they find it almost impossible to function in the real world. I've met others who are so far gone they've forgotten about personal hygiene." She grinned. "At least we still take baths, although lately I have to confess mine have gotten shorter because it's so late when I get back to my room."

The cold air had pinkened her cheeks and her eyes sparkled with an excitement that once again stirred guilt inside him.

He'd been driving her hard, forcing her to work longer hours than he normally worked. Had he subconsciously been trying to punish her for long-ago transgressions?

"Look, I'm sorry I've been pushing you so hard this week," he said.

"It's all right." She leaned over and touched the back of his hand lightly. She was a toucher. That was one of the things he'd forgotten about her, one of the things he'd been reminded of about her.

"Nate, I know what's at stake here and I don't mind putting in long hours, but after so many hours my brain shuts off. Maybe you don't need the balance of something besides work, but I do."

"I'll keep that in mind for future reference," he replied.

"So, tell me where we're going? I'm positively starving."

He thought perhaps it wasn't just food she was hungry for, but that she was also starving for a different environment, variety and conversation that had nothing to do with a computer program.

"The Boston Beanery," he replied. "It's a great restaurant. I still meet my parents there occasionally for a meal."

"How are your parents?"

"Fine, I guess."

"You guess?"

"I haven't spoken to them in several weeks," he said.

"Really?"

"They're very busy people." He was surprised to hear a defensive edge to his own voice. "We just aren't one of those families that speak to each other every day or every other day.''

He turned his attention out the window, not wanting to think about his parents. They were good people and he loved them, but he sometimes felt like an afterthought in their busy lives.

It was about a twenty-minute drive to the restaurant and as the cabby drove, Nate played tourist guide, pointing out spots of interest along the way. She listened intently, asking questions about the city, the people and the history of his hometown. He knew her interest was genuine. There wasn't a fake bone in Kat's body.

When they reached the restaurant, they got out of the cab and started for the front door of the busy establishment.

''Nate?''

He jumped in surprise as she once again touched his hand, this time grabbing it in hers. ''What?'' He kept his hand still in hers, although he had an impulse to turn it palm up and tangle his fingers with hers.

''Let's make a deal—let's not talk about work while we eat, okay?''

''All right,'' he agreed uneasily. If they didn't talk about work, then what on earth would they talk about? he wondered.

He sure didn't want to talk about their shared history, but it had been so long since he'd indulged in any form of small talk, he was afraid he'd forgotten how and for some reason that was not something he wanted her to know about him.

The restaurant was charming. Housed in an old brick building, there were huge kettles of beans bubbling over several open fireplaces.

Tables were placed with a comfortable distance between them, affording diners an aura of privacy despite the fact that the place was large and filled with people.

She felt exhilarated and knew it was because she was out of the office and out of her hotel room. She probably would have been just as happy if he'd chosen to drive her through some cheesy hamburger joint…anything for a break from the tension and silence of working next to him at the computer and the utter quiet and loneliness of her hotel suite.

"Good evening." The waiter was a cute kid with bright blue eyes and the overeagerness of a student subsisting on tips. "How are you folks doing this evening?" he asked as he handed them each a menu.

"Great." She eyed his name tag. "We're doing just great, Jimmy. How about you?"

He looked at her in surprise and flashed a friendly smile. "I'm doing good."

"Are you a student?"

"Yeah, premed at Boston University."

"That's wonderful. I'm sure you'll make a fine doctor," she exclaimed.

He grinned. "But, for tonight I'm just a waiter feeding the hungry masses."

She laughed. "What do you recommend, Jimmy who is going to be a doctor but for tonight is a waiter?"

"Our specialty is our pork chops simmered in a honey-and-mustard sauce and served with our famous molasses and brown sugar beans."

"If that's the specialty, then that's what I want," she said. She closed her menu and handed it to Jimmy, who then turned to Nate.

"Make it two," Nate said. "And a bottle of good white wine." He handed Jimmy his menu and the young man scurried away. Nate leaned back in his seat and eyed her with a touch of amusement.

"What?" she asked.

"I'd forgotten that about you," he replied.

"Forgotten what?"

"How you like to flirt with waiters."

She stared at him in amazement. "I don't flirt with waiters," she protested.

"Then what do you call what you were just doing?"

She sighed in exasperation. Nate looked so uptight, so judgmental. What had happened to the man who had run half-naked next to her on the beach, laughing with abandon as they splashed in the waves? Had he only been a figment of her imagination?

Apparently she'd been with Nate for four months of his life when he'd experienced some sort of breakdown and had actually been fun. "It wasn't flirting, Nate. It's called being friendly, being sociable with other human beings. You got to be pretty good at it when you were in California."

"I did a lot of things when I was in California that I wouldn't choose to do again," he said softly.

"You mean like date me?" She held her breath for a long moment.

He studied her, his green eyes so piercing, so beautiful. It should be a sin for men to have eyes as pretty as his. "What are you doing, Kat? Putting words into my mouth? Trying to pick a fight?"

She bit her tongue as Jimmy appeared with their bottle of wine. With a jaunty flourish he poured them each a glass, then disappeared.

Kat heaved a deep sigh and shoved her glass of wine toward Nate. "I just want water and, no, I'm not trying to pick a fight, Nate. I'd just hate it if you regretted our time together."

He waved a hand dismissively. "Ancient history. No regrets. Do you still surf?"

It was an obvious attempt to change the subject and Kat decided to let it go. What good could come out of rehashing their past?

They'd been two very different people with two very different ideas of what life was about who'd shared a speck of time pretending that they weren't different at all.

And maybe deep inside she had been trying to pick a fight, evoke emotions that would somehow break up the tension that had simmered just beneath the surface between them from the moment she'd arrived.

"Yeah, I still surf, although not as often as I used to. Soon after you left to return here to Boston, my mom came back from Florida and she required a lot of time." She bit her bottom lip, aware that she'd said too much.

"Required a lot of time? Was she ill?"

Her mother and her problems was the single thing in Kat's life she guarded carefully and old defenses instantly kicked in. "No, she was fine. She just... she'd missed me and wanted to spend a lot of time with me."

She took a sip of her water and looked down at the table, unable to sustain the little white lie and look him in the eyes at the same time.

"Do you still live at the beach house?"

"No. It got too crazy even for me. I lost track of who lived there and who didn't. There was never any privacy and too much partying going on. Once my business started to take off I bought myself a little condo. It's small, but it's all mine. I understand you've got a condo, too."

"Yes. Where I lived seemed more important to my mother than to me, so she found it for me." He took a sip of his wine. "It's really too big just for me, but it's home."

She knew only a little about his parents. During their time together in California, he'd spoken infrequently about them, but from what little he'd said, she'd managed to get a feel for them.

She knew they were both highly esteemed history professors at Boston University, both published frequently in their fields and part of the respectable old guard of Boston.

Their meals arrived and for a few minutes they focused on the delicious food and fell silent. The sounds of other diners talking and the rattle of dishes and glasses as the busboys and waiters worked was comforting. The sounds of life, after a full week of near silence filled her with exuberance.

Even when she was working in her home office, she rarely worked in silence. She'd have the radio blaring or a talk show on television. Noise. Sound. Life.

"If you aren't surfing anymore, what else do you do besides work and visit with your mother?" he asked between bites.

"Go out with friends, go to the movies and things like that. I took a culinary class for two months."

One of his dark eyebrows danced upward. "You learned how to cook?"

She grinned. "No, I flunked miserably. I'm back to eating microwavable dinners and dining in fine drive-through restaurants most of the time. What about you? Have you ever learned to cook?"

He shook his head. "I'm never home long enough to worry about cooking."

"And eventually you'll have a little lady at home

to do all your cooking for you,'' she said, surprised to discover that the thought of Nate having the perfect homemaking wife bothered her just a bit.

''That's the plan,'' he agreed.

''Got anyone in mind?''

''Nobody in particular. There hasn't been time to meet anyone. Planning and developing Utopia has taken up all my time and energy.'' He took another sip of his wine, his gaze holding hers intently. ''What about you? Is there a Mr. Right in your life?''

''No, no Mr. Right. And unfortunately, you weren't the last of my Mr. Wrongs.'' The confession evoked a tiny ache inside her heart. There hadn't been a lot of men in her life, but she'd gone into each relationship hopeful that it would be the one—the last—that the man she was dating would fill her heart and soul. Nate had come the closest, until he'd told her what he expected from her.

''Sorry to hear that,'' he said.

''What? That I've dated a lot of Mr. Wrongs?'' She laughed. ''Don't be sorry. Haven't you heard the old saying about having to kiss a lot of frogs before you find Prince Charming?''

She wondered, how many toads he had kissed since they'd parted? She had a feeling there had not been many and she didn't know if that made her pleased or sad.

Chapter Five

Nate had been worried about what they would find to talk about, but he realized he shouldn't have worried. Kat was a natural-born talker, an entertainer with stories and vignettes of life that were both amusing and thought-provoking.

They lingered after the meal, drinking coffee and chatting, her doing most of the chatting. She told him about some of her more colorful clients, making him laugh. The laughter felt good.

That was the gift she'd given him years ago—his laughter. Then she'd stolen it away. He shoved the thought away, not wanting intrusions from the past to spoil their evening.

"I've even worked with the local police department on occasion," she said.

"On security issues?"

She shook her head. "Actually, I work for them as a decoy. I pretend to be a twelve-year-old girl or boy and go into chat rooms to monitor for suspected pedophiles."

"Isn't that dangerous?" he asked.

"Not really. If I connect with a suspected pedophile, I set up a meet and then the cops send a police officer who looks like she's about ten years old and specializes in face-to-face meetings. I don't charge the police. I consider it my donation of community service."

"I was about ten when I started spending all my time on a computer," he said. "Of course, at that time there weren't any chat rooms or anything to worry about."

"Why were you on a computer at ten years old and not out climbing trees or playing football with the local kids?"

Nate sipped his coffee thoughtfully. "My parents frowned on sports and encouraged me to seek academic pursuits in my spare time. I learned at a very early age that the way to get my parents' approval was to work hard and learn well."

"That's all well and good, but surely you had friends that came over, did the usual boyhood things that boys do."

He took another sip of his coffee, the conversation making him uncomfortable. He wasn't accustomed to talking about himself, especially his childhood. "Sure. I'll bet you had a houseful of friends at your place when you were young." It was a conscious attempt to get the subject away from himself and back to her.

To his surprise she gazed down into her coffee mug and wrapped her hands around it. She looked lovely with the flicker of the candle in the center of the table illuminating her features.

She'd always had the smooth complexion that begged touching and the years hadn't changed that. His fingers itched to lightly trace down her cheek, feel the soft silk of her skin.

He'd expected her to laugh and tell him that their house had been like Grand Central Station, kids running in and out, laughing and bonding as only young kids could do. Instead, when she raised her eyes and looked at him, he saw dark shadows that spoke of distant pain.

"I had friends in and out of the house until I was eight, then after my father left us, my mother sort of fell apart. She'd built her whole life around my father and then suddenly he was gone and everything changed."

He leaned forward, intrigued by the darkness in her eyes. He'd never seen it before. During their time in California, her eyes had always been filled with light and laughter. "What do you mean, everything changed?"

She looked down into her cup again and this time when she looked back at him the shadows that had darkened her beautiful hazel eyes were gone. "Oh you know, she was depressed and so I stopped bringing my friends around. It was no big deal, I just spent a lot of time at my friends' houses instead of bringing my friends home.''

Somehow he had a feeling there was more to the story than what she'd just offered, but she seemed to have no inclination to divulge any more and he didn't intend to press her on the matter. After all, what did he care what kind of childhood she'd had? He certainly didn't like to talk about his own.

''I don't know about you, but I'm exhausted,'' she said as she shoved her now-empty coffee cup to the side.

''Yeah, I'm ready to go.''

Within minutes they had paid the tab, left the restaurant and were back in the seat of a cab taking them to her hotel. ''This was nice, Nate. Thank you,'' she said.

''I enjoyed it, too,'' he confessed. She sat close enough to him that their thighs touched and, even through the material of their clothing and coats, he thought he could feel the heat of her skin.

''You aren't planning on going back to the office tonight, are you?''

''I was thinking about it. I figured I could get in a few more hours of work.''

She looked concerned. ''Why don't you just go home, Nate. Sleep in your own bed in your own house. We can get started again early in the morning.'' She touched his arm. ''Surely your bed at home is more comfortable than sleeping slumped over your computer keyboard.''

''You're right, I'll probably just go home tonight.'' It was difficult for him to concentrate on the conversation with her sitting so close.

''Nate.'' Her hand moved down his arm to light on his hand. ''I know how important this project is to you, and how important our work to find the problem is, but I can't keep up the pace that you set the last week indefinitely.''

Her hand was warm as it rested lightly on his and he wanted to turn his hand palm up and twine his fingers with hers. He moved his hand away from her touch so he couldn't follow through on his desire.

''I know, I've been pushing us both too hard,'' he agreed.

She settled back in the seat, her thigh moving away from his. The absence of her warmth made it easier for him to think. ''I'd like to meet your tech team. Would that be possible?'' she asked.

''Sure, I can take you to meet them tomorrow.''

Their conversation halted as the cab pulled up in front of her hotel. He got out, then extended a hand to help her from the back seat. He paid the driver then turned back to her. ''It's late. I'll walk you to your room.''

''That isn't necessary,'' she replied.

''I don't mind. Besides, it will give me an opportunity to work off a little of that meal.''

She smiled at him. "Then maybe we should take the stairs."

"What floor are you on?"

"The twelfth."

He returned her smile. "The elevator it is."

As they stepped into the awaiting elevator, she looked up at him. "It's funny, isn't it? That when we were seeing each other in California, we never really talked about ourselves...our families or our pasts."

"That thought crossed my mind earlier," he replied. He shrugged. "We never seemed to lack for conversation, though."

"That's true." She fell silent as the door opened on the twelfth floor. "My room is this way." She gestured to the left, then dug into her purse and produced a room-card key.

She stopped in front of her door and he took the key from her and inserted it into the slot. When the green light flickered on, she pushed the door open and took the key back from him. "You always were a gentleman, Nate. Thanks again for a lovely evening, even if I did have to stomp my feet and curse a little to get it."

Her face was tilted up to him, her eyes seemed to beckon him and her lips looked dewy and soft. Without conscious thought, following only a need that was suddenly ravenous, he bent down and touched his lips to hers.

Immediately her mouth opened to him, and the kiss became more, far more than the mere meeting of two sets of lips. His tongue slid into her mouth and danced with hers as blood pumped desire through his veins.

He wasn't sure if she broke the kiss or he did. He only knew that they stood facing each other, her cheeks flushed and her eyes wide with surprise.

"Why did you do that?" she asked, her voice slightly breathless.

Why, indeed? Why in the heck had he done that? He shoved his hands into his coat pockets, irritated by the unexpected impulse that had driven him to kiss her. "I don't know...habit, I guess."

"Habit?" Her eyebrow arched slightly above her right eye. "Habit after five years?"

He shrugged. "I guess some old habits die harder than others. Good night, Kat." Before she could say anything else, he turned on his heels and headed for the elevator.

He kept his mind blank until he hit the outside air and began the walk back to the office building where his car was in the underground parking lot. Only then did he allow himself to wonder what had possessed him to kiss her.

Had it been the novelty of taking time off, eating in a restaurant and indulging in talk that had nothing to do with his work?

Had it been the fact that for a few minutes, as he'd watched her in that soft, complimentary candlelight, the years had faded away and he'd felt happy...lighter hearted, like he'd felt before when he'd been in her company.

The outside air, bitterly cold and smelling of a pending new bout of snow, did nothing to cool the heat that fired through his body as he thought of that kiss.

For months after he'd left California and returned to Boston, he'd dreamed of the kisses he'd shared with Kat. He'd dreamed of her soft lips, open and yielding to him, just as they had been moments before.

He had to get the thought of that kiss out of his head. He had to make sure he didn't give in to such a stupid impulse again.

Kat was hired help, nothing more, nothing less. He had to remember that she was simply a woman who had been brought in to help him solve the Utopia problem. When the problem was solved, she'd go back to California and the odds were good their paths would never cross again.

That kiss. It haunted her all night long, bringing back memories she didn't want to remember, memories she'd worked hard to forget.

Damn the man. He was such an enigma, brilliant in so many ways, but old-fashioned and stupid in others. He was such a…such a man!

Kat tried to shove him out of her mind as she took a fast shower, got into her nightshirt and climbed into bed. But he refused to exit her thoughts.

She hadn't missed how adroitly he'd changed the subject when she'd been asking questions about his childhood. What little he'd shared with her had been troubling.

His words had painted a picture of a lonely young boy who only achieved his parents' approval through academic success and nothing else. Not exactly a picture-perfect childhood.

She slammed a fist into her pillow, flopped down on her back and closed her eyes. She hadn't exactly had an ideal childhood, either, but she'd survived and apparently Nate was doing just fine.

That kiss. He was dangerous with his kisses. The last thing she wanted was to pick up their relationship where they had left off five years ago.

Long after Nate had left California, she'd realized that their relationship had been one based on lust. She had tumbled into bed with him far too quickly and the passion between them had remained intense for the four months they had dated.

That's really all they'd had—passion. Kat knew passion was important in a relationship, but it took far more than that to make a relationship last forever. And that's what she was looking for now—a forever kind of relationship.

She had finally reached a place in her life where she would consider marriage to the right man a possibility. The only problem was finding the right man, and she knew Nate Leeman was simply a toad who kissed very, very well.

She awakened early the next morning, once again in time to see another beautiful Boston sunrise. If she'd been at home she would have carried a cup of coffee out on her deck where she could hear the sounds of the ocean.

Her first instinct was to shower quickly and get right to the office, but instead she ordered up a room service breakfast and, after eating, took a long, leisurely bath.

Although Nate had admitted he'd been driving them both hard and had indicated he'd take it easier from here on, she didn't believe him.

Nate was driven, obsessed with work and, from what she'd seen in the past week, a man without any other life. He'd be back to being a slave driver by the end of today. She knew it was important that she assert herself and let him know she would work the hours that were most comfortable for her.

It was just after eight when she walked into the office door, unsurprised to find Nate already at his computer monitor.

"Good morning," she said cheerfully as she took off her coat.

"Somebody wreaked havoc in the past twenty-four hours," he said, not looking away from the monitor.

Her stomach plunged to her toes. "What's going on?"

"More segments changed...sabotaged actually, screwed up enough that if I hadn't found the changes, the program would be rendered useless. I think I've just about got them all corrected, but I need to read through it again to see."

She sat down and leaned over so she could see his monitor, see the area of the program where he'd been working. "Were the segments copied before the changes were made?" He nodded. "Any way to tell how they broke in?"

"I haven't taken the time to look. My main concern has been to fix the damage."

Kat powered up her own system and pulled up the program. "Then while you do damage control, I'll look for evidence of how they got in."

For the next couple of hours they worked silently, focused only on the task at hand. Nate's phone rang once and, after a brief conversation with somebody on the other end of the line, he buzzed his secretary and told her to hold all other calls, that he couldn't be disturbed.

It was just after noon when Nate finally sighed in relief and shoved back from his desk. "I think I've fixed it all."

Kat sighed as well, only hers was one of frustration. "And I still can't find a back door that would allow an outside source to get in." She pushed back from her desk and stood, then stretched with arms overhead.

She was unaware of her blouse riding up with her motion until she saw Nate staring at her midsection. She quickly put her arms down and tugged at the bottom of her blouse as Nate strode toward the minibar.

"I'm having a drink," he exclaimed. "What can I get you? A Scotch and water? A Bloody Mary?"

"Nothing." She walked over to the sofa and sat. "Actually, if you have any bottled water in the refrigerator, I'll take one of those."

She watched as he fixed himself a light Scotch and water, then grabbed a bottle of water and carried them both to where she sat. He handed her the water, then sat next to her, a curious look on his face. "Now that I think about it, you never had an alcoholic drink when we were in California together."

She nodded and twisted off the top of the water bottle. "I don't drink." She hesitated a moment, wanting to make sure she wanted him to know what she was about to say. She finally decided it didn't really matter, not anymore. "My mother was an alcoholic...a bad one."

"Oh, I'm sorry. I didn't know."

She took a sip of her water, then leaned back against the buttery-soft sofa. "After my father left, she was so depressed, so hopeless, and that's when she began to drink. At first it wasn't too bad. She'd at least wait until noon. It got worse and worse."

It was as if she'd opened Pandora's box. Once she began talking about it, she couldn't seem to stop. She had never shared this with anyone, ever, but at this moment the words spewed out of her like steam from a pressure cooker.

"I was afraid to bring friends home from school. I never knew what to expect when I walked through the door of our house. Some days I'd come home and she'd be fine, puttering in the kitchen or cleaning the place up. Other times I came home to find her passed out or drunk as a skunk, reeling around, breaking things and screaming about my father.''

Old emotions swept through her along with painful memories. Her mother passed out on the floor of the living room half-naked, her mother passed out in the bathtub, her mother raving and screaming in drunken rages, cursing the fact that she'd built her life around her husband and he'd taken her life away when he'd gone.

''Why didn't you tell me any of this before?'' Nate asked and set his drink on the coffee table. He reached out, as if to embrace her, but it was a tentative gesture and she knew how difficult it must have been for him to make.

She shrugged and he dropped his hands. ''I was ashamed and afraid. At the time I was seeing you, Mom wasn't living in Florida. She was in a rehab center in Arizona. I was so afraid it wouldn't work, that she'd come back and things would be the same. And I was afraid to tell you because I thought it would make you leave me.''

He took her hand in his. ''How could you think that about me?''

She smiled wryly. ''I knew that you weren't exactly Boston trash, that your family had money and prestige and a level of respectability that few attain.

I couldn't tell you that my mother was a drunk and was on an extended stay at a rehab center.''

"How long was she there?"

"Four months. They not only offered her help with her addiction, but also counseling for her self-esteem and job training.''

"Must have been expensive," he said.

"Dreadfully expensive. Dad had left Mom a settlement when he walked out the door. She'd refused to touch it, had called it his guilt money. I convinced her to use it to get help.''

"Did it work?"

She smiled. "She's been clean and sober for five years. It's been the best years of my life with her. We're best friends and there's nothing better than seeing her happy and healthy. She has a job she loves as a legal secretary, has a flower garden that the neighbors envy and has finally found peace and acceptance within herself.''

His gaze held hers, his normally piercing green eyes more gentle. "I'm glad. I just wish you would have told me this before.''

The softness in his eyes was dangerous, as was his closeness to her. Bringing up those painful memories of her childhood made her want to be held, as she'd never been held when she'd been going through those horrendous days and nights.

Abruptly she stood and moved away from where he sat on the sofa. She stood with her back to him. "I couldn't tell you then. I wasn't ready to share it with anyone. Besides, it wouldn't have made any difference in anything.''

She turned to face him and forced a smile. ''We really weren't into deep confidences when we were together before. We were into having fun...passing time and having sex.'' Her cheeks flushed slightly at the shallow characterization of what they had shared.

His jaw muscles tightened and he picked up his glass and drained it in two swallows. ''You're right and we've passed enough time now that we should get back to work.''

He stood and returned to his desk. She knew she'd irritated him by her assessment of their past. She'd cheapened it, belittled the feelings they'd had for each other. But it was better that way.

It was better that she believe it was no big deal than to remember the heartache she'd experienced when he'd told her what he'd wanted from her, what he'd expected from her when he'd proposed to her.

They worked until six, tension back in the air between them. She'd hoped their time away from work the night before would have eased some of the tension between them. Instead, it was as if the pleasant evening had never happened.

He was terse, snapping answers to any questions she might have and cranky with anyone who stepped into the office for anything.

By six-thirty that evening she'd had enough. She shut down her computer terminal and stood. He looked up at her questioningly. "What are you do-ing?"

"Calling it a night. I told you last night I didn't intend to work the same crazy hours that you do." She reached into the closet and pulled out her coat. "I thought you were going to introduce me to some of the tech team members today."

He stood. "I forgot all about it."

"I'd really rather meet them in an informal kind of setting rather than here while they work. What do you think about me setting up a little party in my hotel suite for them."

"That isn't necessary. They meet every Friday night at a little tavern not far from here. If you want, this Friday we can go there and I'll introduce you around."

"That would be perfect...thanks." She put on her coat and got her gloves out of her pocket. He headed toward the closet, but she stopped him with a hand on his arm. "If you're getting your coat to walk me to my hotel, please don't."

"But it's growing dark. You shouldn't be out on the street alone," he protested.

"Nate, I'm thirty-one years old. I've virtually been on my own since I was eight. I'm perfectly capable of walking a few blocks by myself. Besides, I could use a little solitude."

His eyes radiated surprise. "All right, then."

She dropped her hand from his arm. "I'll see you tomorrow."

"What are you going to do about dinner?" he asked.

"I'll just order up some room service. I'm really tired."

"I could take you out."

She shook her head. "Not tonight. But I may take you up on the offer for dinner tomorrow night."

"Okay, then I guess I'll see you in the morning."

She fled the office, unsure why she felt the need to be away from him. She felt vulnerable, far too vulnerable to eat with him, to spend another moment with him.

The uneasiness between them all day had been different than what she'd experienced the week before. All last week she'd gotten the distinct impression that part of the tension was because he didn't want her here, was angry that an outsider had been brought into his project.

She'd also been smart enough to recognize that there was some baggage from their previous relationship. She'd understood that, and she'd thought they'd gotten past that the night before at dinner.

But this tension was as much hers as it was his. All day long the thought of his kiss had intruded into her thoughts, stirring a desire inside her she'd thought long dead.

She stepped out of the office building and headed toward her hotel. It had been the spill of secrets that had made her feel so vulnerable and that moment when he'd raised his arms as if to embrace her, that moment when he'd taken her hand in his.

She knew Nate was not naturally a demonstrative person, that casual touching and affectionate hugging had always been difficult for him. The fact that he'd offered his arms to her had touched her deeply...too deeply.

The job. That was all that was important and she had to focus on that and forget the sweet, hot kiss they'd shared the night before, forget any previous relationship she'd had with Nate before walking into his Boston office.

Chapter Six

Nate stood at the window and stared out at the snow that fell from the gray skies. It was early morning and he didn't expect Kat in for another hour or so.

She'd remained firm about the hours she worked. She came in around eight, took an hour lunch at noon, then worked until six or seven and called it a night.

Twice in the past week he had taken her to dinner. He told himself he was simply doing his job, treating a fellow co-worker well, but the truth was he'd enjoyed those dinners with her.

She made him see the world differently. She made it seem like an enchanted wonderland where everything was new and exciting. That had been her charm before, and she hadn't lost it.

He'd been shocked by her background. She'd always seemed so centered, so sure of herself and where she was going in life. Nobody would have guessed at the chaos that had apparently been her childhood.

There had been no chaos in his childhood. His had been one of order, structure. No noise, no fuss, no messy emotions. He frowned thoughtfully and realized it had been too long since he'd last checked in with his parents.

His parents were early risers. By this time they would be finishing up their morning coffee at the kitchen table, preparing to go to the university for morning classes.

He left the window and sat at his desk, then picked up the phone and punched in their number. It rang three times before it was answered. "Leeman residence," a pleasant female voice said.

"Mrs. Richards, it's Nate."

"How are you, Mr. Nate?"

"Fine, just fine." Nate didn't know the housekeeper well. She was the latest in a long string of people who had worked for his parents at one time or another. "Is my mother or father home?"

"No, they're gone. They left on research leave last week. You just caught me here watering the plants and checking on things."

"Research leave? How long are they going to be gone?" Nate felt a heaviness in his chest as he realized they'd taken off without a word of goodbye. He didn't know why it bothered him this time. It had certainly happened often enough in the past.

"Three months," Mrs. Richards replied. "They plan to be out of the country until the end of March."

"Where did they go?"

"Someplace in England. I can't remember offhand, but if you'll hold a minute I have their itinerary in my purse."

"No, no, that's all right," Nate said hurriedly. "I'm sure I'll hear from them sometime in the next couple of days. Thanks, Mrs. Richards."

He murmured a goodbye, then hung up.

Three months.

They wouldn't be here when Utopia was unveiled and made public. They wouldn't be here to see his success, to revel in his accomplishment.

Big deal, he told himself. He shoved away from the desk and went back to stare out into the gray beginning of the day. He was thirty-one years old. He didn't exactly need his mommy and daddy to be at his side.

Still, it would have been nice, he thought. It would have been nice if just once his father had clapped him on the back with pride shining from his eyes. It would have been nice if just once his mother had pulled him into a loving embrace. It would have been nice if just once he felt as if he mattered to the people who had raised him.

The office door flew open and he jerked around to see Kat breezing in. She filled the room with her presence as she flashed him a bright smile. "It's supposed to snow a couple more inches.'' She shrugged out of her coat. "I love it!"

"I'm sick of it," he replied.

"Hmm, somebody must have awakened on the wrong side of the bed this morning," she said with an arched brow. "Or is this just another example of your normal taciturn, sometimes surly moods?"

She looked gorgeous. She wore a copper-colored skirt and jacket with a beige blouse. Gold earrings gleamed at her ears and a heavy gold necklace added a dash of flashy elegance.

The copper clothing emphasized the coppery highlights of her auburn hair, and her cheeks were rosy from her encounter with the outside elements.

The sarcastic retort he'd been about to utter died on his lips and instead he raked a hand through his hair and sank down on the sofa. "I just got a bit of news that disappointed me. Sorry if I snapped at you."

"It's all right." She sat next to him and placed a hand on his knee. Always touching, it was as if she couldn't help herself. "Want to talk about it?"

He stared down at her hand, noting the pretty polish that colored her short, square-trimmed nails. She smelled like snow and fresh, clean woman and desire for her hit him square in the gut.

No, he didn't want to talk about it. He didn't even want to think about it anymore. He placed his hand over hers, enjoying the feel of her warm, soft skin.

"You were beautiful five years ago, but I think you're even more beautiful now."

Her eyes widened in surprise at his words and her mouth opened just enough for him to take the gesture as an invitation.

Before he could second-guess himself or her, he leaned forward and took her lips with his.

She remained stiff and unmoving for a long moment, then her fingers tangled with his and she leaned toward him.

He placed his free hand on the back of her head, loving the way the silky strands of her hair seemed to curl intimately around his fingers. He'd always loved the feel of her soft, thick hair.

The kiss deepened as she broke their hand embrace and faced him more squarely. She wrapped her arms around him and gave herself fully to the kiss.

With their tongues battling, he leaned her back until they were half-lying on the sofa, her breasts pressed firmly against his chest.

The intimate contact evoked memories that stroked his desire even higher, hotter. He remembered each and every time he'd made love to her in their four months together. The energy, the excitement and the laughter between them had been addictive.

Whenever he'd made love to her he'd felt at peace…complete. She'd filled him up as no woman had before, or since.

He wanted that again, right here, right now. She

gave no indication that she didn't want the same thing.

He broke the kiss and trailed his lips down her jaw and to the hollow of her throat. Her scent surrounded him and he loved the taste of her skin.

Her breathing came in a catchy, breathy rhythm that he remembered from years ago. The sound of it rocketed desire through him.

His mouth took hers once again and he forgot the fact that they were in his office where anyone could walk in at any time. He forgot everything except the heat and sweetness of Kat.

He imagined he could feel the heat of her hands radiating through his suit jacket and shirt, but rationally knew that was impossible. He wanted to feel the heat of her. He wanted her naked beneath him, his skin loving hers.

He wanted what they'd had before, wanted to make love to her until they were both breathless and spent and utterly sated. Then, he wanted to linger with her in his arms, fall asleep with her sleeping beside him.

It wasn't until his hand sought the warmth of her skin beneath her blouse that she murmured a soft protest.

"Nate." It was just a whisper, but it was enough to bring him back to reality, return common sense to his brain. They were in his office, where anyone could walk in at any time. What had he been thinking?

Reluctantly he sat up and pulled her to a sitting position as well. Her lips were slightly puffy from his kisses and she looked as if she was coming out of a deep sleep.

As the daze in her eyes cleared, she stood and straightened her blouse and jacket. "I'm not sure what that was all about, but I'll be more careful about the place and time that I ask you if you want to talk about anything."

Embarrassment swept over him as he realized how easily he'd succumbed to his weakness, and that Kat had always been his weakness.

"I apologize," he said stiffly. He stood and straightened his tie, wishing he was anyplace but standing beneath her steady scrutiny.

"No need to apologize," she replied. "You just surprised me, that's all."

"I surprised myself," he admitted. He moved to his desk. "Shall we get to work?"

He was making her crazy, Kat thought four hours later as she left Nate's office and headed for the company cafeteria. She enjoyed the noise and chatter of the cafeteria.

She got in line with her thoughts still filled with Nate. He could blow as hot as a desert breeze and as cold as an arctic wind, and she never knew for sure what to expect.

When she'd first entered the office that morning his beautiful eyes had held an expression she'd never seen before—a deep, abiding sadness that she'd felt resonate momentarily inside her as well.

The last thing she'd expected was to end up on the sofa desperately wanting him to make love to her. But the moment his lips had touched hers, that's what she'd wanted.

It had taken every ounce of her willpower to stop him before they did something she knew they would both regret. She refused to consider falling back into the same kind of relationship they'd had before, where lovemaking had been too easy and really getting to know each other had been too difficult.

When they had gotten to work, silence had reigned between them—an uncomfortable silence that had made her want to scream or curse or slap him into displaying some kind of emotion besides cool, calm competence.

She entered the cafeteria and waved to several people she'd gotten acquainted with over the past week of eating lunch there.

After she'd gotten her food she carried her tray to a table where her new friends had motioned her over.

"Bad morning?" Janie, who worked in the mail room, looked at her sympathetically.

"Does it show?" Kat set her tray down on the table then sat on the chair next to the young girl.

"It's Leeman stress," Becky, a secretary from the sales department explained. "Nate Leeman might be a handsome cuss but he has nothing but ice water in his veins."

No, not ice water, Kat thought as she remembered

the kisses they'd shared earlier that morning. Nate had red-hot blood rushing through his veins.

He had deep passion and the capacity for laughter, but he kept those traits trapped inside him and allowed them out all too infrequently.

"I once made a play for him," Janie confessed. "I mean, he is handsome. He looked at me like I was crazy."

"If you had a monitor screen instead of a face, he'd probably marry you in a minute," Becky replied, making them all laugh.

The rest of the lunch passed with girl chatter. Kat listened as the rest of them bemoaned their men problems, whined about parent problems and shared child-rearing secrets.

Most of these women had it all, Kat thought. Although they griped and complained, it was about superficial things, not about big issues. For the most part they had loving husbands, good careers and adorable children. They were proof positive that women could juggle a career and a family and keep all the balls in the air.

"What about you, Kat? Is marriage in your future?" Janie asked.

"Yeah, tell us the truth. You probably have some gorgeous California surfer dude panting after you," Becky said.

Kat laughed. "California surfer dudes have been slightly overrated. I'm sure there are some great ones out there, but I always seem to find the ones that have obviously swallowed too much salt water.''

The others laughed, then Becky looked at her more seriously. "So, no mad, passionate love affair in your life?"

Kat speared a carrot from her salad and tried not to think of the kisses she'd shared with Nate hours before. "No, not at the moment. I had one a long time ago, but it ended badly." Even now, after all the years that had passed, the relationships she'd had since, the pain of her breakup with Nate still lingered.

"Oh, hon, men are such pigs," Betty, exclaimed. She was older than the others, had recently gone through a bitter divorce and Kat wasn't clear where she worked in the corporation.

"Now, Betty, you can't judge all men by your ex," Becky replied.

Nate hadn't been a pig. Had he been a pig, the pain of their parting wouldn't have remained, Kat thought as she finished her lunch.

Nate had simply been the man she loved, the man who had wanted more from her than she'd been able to give.

After lunch she was headed back to the office when she ran into Emily Winters in the hallway. "Kat, how are things going?" Emily asked.

Kat knew she wasn't talking about life in general, but probably wanted an update on their work. "Too slow as far as Nate is concerned and I'm sure too slow for you and Mr. Winters."

Emily smiled. "Dad and I both know you're doing the best you can."

Kat noticed the pretty, painted trinket box she held in her hand. "Nice," Kat said.

Emily looked at the box and slowly nodded. "I have a collection of them. My ex-husband just brought me this one to add to my collection."

"That was nice."

Emily looked at the delicate piece, then back at Kat with a grin. "He's nicer to me now than he was when we were married. It makes me wonder about him."

Her smile faded. "Hopefully you and Nate can figure this out soon. The date of the release of the program is approaching fast."

Kat hesitated a minute, then decided to go ahead and tell her what she and Nate had concluded just before lunch. "I can tell you this. We don't think it's a hacker."

Emily's vivid blue eyes were puzzled. "What do you mean? Somebody is getting into the program and copying it and changing things."

"We think it's an inside job."

A tiny gasp left Emily's lips. "Oh, no. What makes you think so?"

"We can't find anyplace where the security measures Nate wrote into the program have been breached. We now believe that whoever is accessing the program and wreaking havoc is doing so through legitimate access. In other words, they're using a recognized password and sliding in and out undetected."

"A recognized password. So it has to be either a tech or somebody who has been assigned their own password."

Kat nodded.

"This is going to break my father's heart," she murmured more to herself than to Kat. "What do we do? What do you need from me?"

"Nothing at the moment."

"I guess we should break the news to my father this afternoon?"

"Actually, I'd rather wait until Monday morning if that's all right with you," Kat said. "Nate and I are meeting the tech team tonight for drinks. I'd like to see them all in an informal setting, talk to them and see if I can get a clue as to who might have a reason to either sabotage or sell portions of the program."

"This is pretty big news, but I guess it wouldn't hurt to wait until Monday to tell my father your findings. Why don't we plan a meeting at eight o'clock Monday morning. We can break the news to him then."

Kat nodded. "And hopefully at that time we'll have a more definitive conclusion of who is responsible. Nate and I are checking time logs now, trying to pinpoint each date and time the program was accessed. Once we have that all logged in, we should be able to check it against work records to see who was working at the time the program was changed or copied."

"It sounds like you and Nate are on top of things,"

Emily said, but to Kat she looked and sounded distracted.

"I'd better get back into the office or Nate will send the National Guard to find me and get me back in my chair," Kat said.

This earned her a conspiratorial smile from Emily. "He can be a bit difficult, can't he?"

Kat grinned. "He's obsessive, a know-it-all, a slave driver and absolutely brilliant." She said goodbye to Emily and hurried down the hallway to his office.

Emily went directly to her office and sat down, the delicate, hand-painted trinket box on the desk before her. Todd had surprised her at lunch, making one of his impromptu visits and bringing her the gift. He'd told her he'd seen it in a boutique and had thought of her and her collection.

She'd accepted it reluctantly, wondering what he was up to. Even when she'd been married to him he hadn't been big on gifts or surprises. Her initial feeling was that he was making a definite attempt to patch things up between them and try for a second chance with her.

She leaned back in her chair and closed her eyes, replaying Kat's words in her head. Her father had founded this company based on integrity and loyalty. He treated his employees well and fostered the image that while they were a large, highly successful company, they were also a kind of family.

It would kill him to learn there was a traitor within their midst.

A knock on her door pulled her from her thoughts. Carmella opened the door and peeked inside. "You okay?"

Emily smiled fondly. "Do you have some sort of internal barometer for people with troubled thoughts?"

"Sure, the arthritis in my knee acts up whenever I see somebody I care about looking unhappy. Want to talk about it?"

Emily motioned her into the chair opposite her desk. "I'll tell you something, but I don't want you to share it with my father yet." Quickly she briefed Carmella on what Kat had told her.

"Oh, my." Carmella sat back in the chair and shook her head. "Your father will be quite upset if that's the case. Who has passwords to access the program?"

"My father and me…and of course Nate. I'm not sure how many of his tech people were assigned to work on the Utopia program. Apparently Kat and Nate are going out for drinks with some of the tech team and Kat wants to check them out before we tell Dad anything. They're also putting together a log of times and dates when the program was changed or copied."

"Sounds like they know what they're doing," Carmella said.

Emily nodded, her attention on the trinket box on

her desk. "Lately it seems that Todd is spending more time here than when he actually worked here." She ran a finger over the glazed top of the little box.

Carmella leaned forward, her dark eyes troubled. "Surely you aren't thinking that Todd has anything to do with the Utopia problems?"

"No, of course not," Emily replied, but disturbing thoughts were suddenly whirling around in her head.

Moments later, after Carmella had left her office, she leaned her head back and closed her eyes, thinking of the man who had once been her husband.

Todd had been overbearing, demanding and difficult as a husband, but he'd never shown any signs of being dishonest or disloyal. He certainly didn't have a password to access the Utopia files.

But he'd worked at Wintersoft, Inc. at one time, had been a trusted husband and son-in-law. He would know where Emily and her father kept their passwords.

He didn't have a job and was maybe more desperate than he indicated, but even knowing this, Emily found it difficult to seriously contemplate that he could be responsible.

Her father had been disappointed when Emily and Todd's marriage hadn't worked out. He would be devastated if it came out that Todd, the man he'd always treated as a son-in-law, was the traitor.

She hoped Kat and Nate came up with the culprit soon, before she had to mention to her father any suspicions she might have about Todd.

Chapter Seven

Wiley's Tavern was walking distance from the Wintersoft, Inc. offices. Although Nate offered to get a cab to take them there, Kat insisted they walk. She seemed to thrive in the cold and snow and so they walked the short distance.

The snow had stopped by noon and the sidewalks had already been cleaned off. Nate had been to Wiley's once, when he'd first started at Wintersoft, Inc. He'd been invited by a co-worker and, being the new man on campus, had decided to accept the invitation.

The place was a typical hole-in-the-wall. Larger on the inside than it looked on the out, Nate had found the place too smoky and noisy and had never gone again. Besides, he'd didn't have time to waste. Even then, Utopia had become more than a thought in his mind, and work was all that was important to him.

"People who live their whole life in sunny California have no idea what they miss by not experiencing snow," Kat said as they walked briskly toward the tavern.

"You always seemed to be such a beach person, I'm surprised you're so enthralled with the snow."

"I've decided in the last couple of weeks that I like them both...snow and beaches." Her eyes sparkled with anticipation and he knew she was looking forward to meeting the crew at the tavern.

Earlier in the day, he'd told her the names of the five techs that had been assigned to the Utopia project, the five that would have passwords and entry into the program at any time of the day or night.

They'd reached the mutual agreement that the breach was internal, not external, that somebody was accessing the program through legitimate means.

"Are you happy here in Boston?" she asked.

He looked at her in surprise. Happy? He never thought much about being happy. "I guess. Boston is my home, it's where I am." He remained focused on her as they walked.

"What made you decide to start your own business? I know at the time we left the school, we both had offers from several of the major players in the computer and business world."

"And I considered each of the offers," she replied, a tiny frown dancing across the center of her forehead. "But, at the time, Mom wasn't out of rehab yet and I didn't know what to expect where she was concerned. I decided to go it alone so I wouldn't be tied to anyone's hours but my own. That way I could be there for Mom whenever she needed me to be.''

''Pretty risky, starting a business.''

She shrugged. ''I figured if it wasn't financially solvent by the end of the first year I could always go back to waiting tables in my spare time to make ends meet.''

She laughed. ''Thankfully, I didn't have to resort to that.'' She kicked at a mound of snow. ''For the most part, I feel as if I'm finally having the kind of life I wanted. My mother is clean and sober, working now and dating a nice man. I have my business, which is challenging and exciting.''

''So, you're living the perfect life, the one you always wanted.'' He was glad she was happy, he told himself. Even when he'd left California with his heart in tatters, he'd never wished unhappiness on her. There was also a small tear in his heart that mended as he recognized that it had been her need to help her mother that had been one of the reasons she hadn't come with him to Boston.

They stopped walking as they reached the door that entered Wiley's Tavern. ''A perfect life...not exactly,'' she said. ''It's a good life, but there are still things I want to make it more complete.'' She broke eye contact with him, but not before he saw what appeared to be a deep yearning cross the hazel depths.

When she looked at him again the emotion was gone, replaced by a carefree sparkle. She linked her arm with his. "Come on, Nate. Let's go inside and have some fun and maybe in the process we'll figure out who is tampering with your baby." With these words she yanked open the tavern door and pulled him inside.

Within minutes they were seated at a large round table near the back of the establishment with the rest of the Utopia tech people. They had all looked shocked when Nate and Kat had walked through the door, but had quickly shifted positions to include the newcomers at their table.

"Here, you can sit here." Roger Barlow held out his chair for Kat. "I was just getting ready to leave anyway."

Everyone protested, but Roger shook his head and grabbed his coat. "I've got a ton of things to do and was going to make it an early night anyway." He left and Kat sat in his place while Nate grabbed an empty chair across the table from her.

For a few minutes the conversation had been stiff and formal and Nate realized he and Kat had put a definite damper on the gathering.

Nate watched as Kat charmed each and every one of them. She did it seemingly effortlessly as not only an avid listener, but an active participant in the conversation.

Soon they became a boisterous group, arguing applications and software designs with passion and intelligence.

Nate had intended to sit back, nurse his Scotch and

soda and watch the interplay of the group. Kat seemed to have other ideas. Again and again she elicited his opinion, sometimes agreeing with it, sometimes vehemently opposing it.

It wasn't just Nate and Kat who argued good-naturedly, but the entire group. There was lots of laughter and, with each moment that passed, Nate felt himself growing more and more relaxed.

He also felt a mixture of other emotions. He regretted that he'd never joined his tech team here before. They were so bright, so full of life and optimism. He knew them only by their work and now he was getting a glimpse of their personalities outside of work and it was a nice experience.

But he hadn't forgotten that it was probable one of them was a traitor, accessing his program, copying portions and sabotaging other sections. He thought of Roger Barlow, who had left almost the moment he and Kat had arrived. His abrupt departure certainly looked a little bit suspicious.

"Are we going to make the release date?" Sam Brubaker leaned over to ask Nate while the others continued to chatter.

"What makes you think we wouldn't?" Nate asked.

Sam, a young man with a shaved bald head and a tongue ring shook his head ruefully. "Boss, you think we don't know what's going on? We've seen the program changes, the copied sectors and if that wasn't enough, the minute we heard that Kathryn Sanderson, aka Tiger Tech, was being called in, we knew there was a security problem.''

''We're on top of it,'' Nate said, hoping he sounded more assured than he felt.

''Good. It would be a damn shame if some piece of garbage screwed things up for the company.''

''Nothing is going to be screwed up,'' Nate replied. He returned his attention to Kat, watching her as she talked to Lily Albright, the only female tech on the team.

Although Nate couldn't hear their conversation, it was obvious Kat was entertaining. Lily was laughing and Kat's eyes sparkled with an impish light.

Nate nursed his second Scotch and soda as the conversation whirled around him. The tavern was noisy, but tonight it didn't bother him. The smoke didn't bother him. Nothing bothered him. He was perfectly content to sit and watch Kat all night long.

It was then he realized he'd never stopped loving her. He loved her as much at this moment as he had five years ago. Even though she had habits that drove him crazy, like eating at her computer and humming off-key when she was deep in concentration, and even though she had broken his heart, he was still in love with her.

The realization filled him with little joy. Rather, the realization sent a sweeping sadness through him. What difference did it make if he loved her? He could love her through eternity, but that didn't change the fact that she wasn't right for him.

They were opposites in everything, from the way they interacted with other people to what they did in their spare time. She was optimistic by nature, he knew he was something of a pessimist. She loved people and Nate was wary of people.

More important than anything, her vision of her future didn't fit what he wanted in his future. Her work was her top priority, and that wasn't the kind of woman he wanted as a wife.

And so his heart would break again when she left Boston and went back to her life in California. It was as inevitable as the bartender serving another drink, as inevitable as cold weather in Boston in January.

He was quiet as they left the tavern. It was after eleven, but Kat seemed as filled with energy as she had when she'd breezed into the office that morning.

"Tell the truth," she said as she linked her arm with his. She smiled up at him and her beauty ached in his chest. "You had fun."

He laughed, unable to help it. "Okay, I had fun," he agreed.

"You should come out and play more often, Mr. Leeman."

"Yeah, I probably should. My team are good people. I knew they were all exceptionally bright, but I didn't realize they were also friendly and filled with enthusiasm. Did you get any vibes from anyone? See any potential defector in the group?"

"Roger Barlow certainly demands a closer look since he flew out the minute we showed up," she said. "He's driving a brand-new car, expensive model."

Nate eyed her in surprise. "How do you know that?"

"Girl talk. Lily is a font of information and I think she has a crush on good old Roger. I'd like to see a personnel file on him, do a little computer sleuthing to check him out."

"What about the others? Sam told me they all know about the program breach."

"They wouldn't be a good tech team if they hadn't noticed the unusual activity," she replied. "Actually, as charming as Lily seemed, I'd like to take a closer look at her, too."

"Why?"

"She mentioned a grandmother in a nursing home, a drain on the family income. She'd be ripe to be bought by another company if the family financial crisis is bad enough."

"You're amazing." He looked down at her. He hadn't thought his respect for her could grow, but it had. "You have a wonderful knack of getting people to trust you, to open up to you."

Her face flushed with the pleasure of his compliment.

"That's because I open up to them. You should try it sometime, Nate. You'd be amazed at the results."

"I'm open," he protested as they passed the office building and continued on their way toward her hotel.

She laughed. "Honestly, Nate. You're about as

open as a clam. Even this morning when I asked you if you wanted to talk about whatever disappointing news you'd received, you didn't want to talk. You kissed me so you wouldn't have to talk...to share.''

"That's not why I kissed you. I kissed you because you looked so pretty, because you looked like you needed to be kissed.''

They stopped in front of her hotel. Kat unlinked her arm from his and stared up at him. "If you really believe that, then not only are you not open to other people, you aren't open to yourself.''

Her words didn't make him mad, but they made him want to prove her wrong. "Trust me, Kat. The reason I kissed you this morning was because I wanted to kiss you. And if you want me to open up, tell you the disappointing news I got this morning, then why don't you invite me up to your room for a nightcap and intimate chat.''

He knew if she invited him into her room, they would make love. Even though he knew there would never be any future with her, he wanted one more time of making love to her, one more memory to burn in his mind, in his heart forever.

Her eyes reflected her hesitation, darkening slightly. If he touched her, took her hand or drew her close to him, she might acquiesce. But he didn't want to pressure her one way or the other. He wanted to make love to her desperately, but only if she wanted it just as much.

"How about we go into the bar and find an intimate

little table, order some coffee and you can open up to me.''

Disappointment swept through him. She apparently wasn't interested in making love to him. He looked at his watch. ''I don't know, maybe I should head on home. It's getting late.''

''It isn't that late,'' she scoffed. ''Nate, you know as well as I do that if we go up to my room we won't talk. Five years ago when we were dating we didn't talk enough and I've always been sorry about that.''

Her words surprised him and sent a warmth of emotion through him that banished the disappointment. She was right. They hadn't talked enough then. ''A cup of coffee sounds good.'' And maybe after they talked, she would invite him up to her room.

A few minutes later Kat and Nate were seated in a booth in a dark corner of the Liberty Bar. The booth forced physical intimacy. Kat could feel the heat of his leg pressed against hers and his shoulder rubbed against hers as he wrapped his hands around the coffee mug before him.

When he'd asked about coming up to her room, she'd had to fight desperately against the weakness that made her want to comply.

She knew if she allowed him into her room that they would go directly to the bed. They would make wild, passionate love and leaving him would be even more difficult than it had been the last time they'd parted.

She knew if she made love to him again, she would be filled with the same rush of emotions he'd evoked in her before, emotions that had only led to heartache.

"The disappointing news I got this morning was that my parents left town last week on a research leave. They'll be gone for the next three months," he said.

Kat eyed him in surprise. "You didn't know they were leaving?"

"No, but that's not really unusual. I'm just disappointed that they won't be here to see the Utopia program unveiled." He stared down into his coffee cup and Kat wasn't sure what to say.

"If it was important to you that they be here, then I'm sorry, Nate," she finally said.

He looked at her, his green eyes radiating a bitterness she'd never seen before. "That's just it. I'm not sure why it's important to me. It shouldn't be. I'm thirty-one years old, it's not like I need their approval."

Although his mouth said one thing, the darkness in his eyes told her another. Kat knew all about the dichotomy of the relationship between parents and children. There had been times in her life when she thought she hated her mother with the same intensity that she loved her.

"Nate, for much of my childhood my mother was a nonfunctioning, falling-down drunk. She was rarely there for me, but that didn't stop me from loving her, from needing her and her approval."

Once again he looked down into his coffee mug. "I don't think my parents should have had a child," he said thoughtfully. "They had their work at the university, their books and research and library. That was their life. They weren't equipped mentally to deal with the needs and the reality of a child."

She reached out and placed her hand over his, surprised to find his skin colder than she'd ever felt it before. In the four months they had dated five years before, he'd never opened himself to her like he was doing at this moment. She felt his vulnerability in the coldness of his hand, saw it in the shadows of his eyes.

"I once came home from school to find my mother naked in the front yard, beating the bushes with a yardstick to get the snakes out. Beat that, Mr. Leeman."

He looked up and shook his head. "I can't." A smile curved one corner of his lips. "We're opposites, Kat, and even our childhood experiences seem to be diametrical."

"Tell me more about yours," she urged, and gave his hand a reassuring squeeze.

"There aren't any real horror stories." He pulled his hand from hers and brought his coffee mug to his lips. He took a drink then returned the mug to the table and drew a deep breath.

"The best way to describe my childhood is silence and isolation. I couldn't have friends in because children were messy, noisy and interfered with my parents' concentration. I wasn't allowed to go to other kids' homes because, according to my parents, I was too smart to consort with average children.''

It was as if a dam had broken. The words tumbled out of him as if they'd been sitting on the end of his tongue just waiting for somebody to ask.

''You know, I'd hear the other kids talking about family stuff, like trips to the zoo, popping popcorn and watching a movie together, cookies and milk after school. I heard about dads wrestling with their sons, mothers cooking special birthday cakes and helping at the kitchen table with homework. It all sounded so wonderful, but it was nothing like what I had.''

''I know the feeling,'' she said softly. ''But, Nate, one of the things I've learned over the years is that it was all about my mother and her weaknesses and in-adequacies. It was never about me.''

She took his hand once again, wondering if he knew that in sharing with her as much as he had, he'd explained so many things about the man he had be-come. ''I used to think that if I could be good enough, if I did everything right, she'd love me enough to stop drinking.''

He nodded. ''And I used to think that if I was smart enough, learned fast enough, I would win their ap-proval, their love and my family would become nor-mal.''

The darkness in his eyes had lightened, as if in telling her about his parents, his past, some of the pain had gone away.

"You know what they say," she said. "That which we survive makes us stronger. Look how far we've both come, Nate. Be proud of yourself. I know I'm proud of myself."

"I just want to get the Utopia program taken care of," he replied. "These last couple of weeks have been so stress-filled." Again a small smile lifted his lips. "If I wasn't under so much stress, I probably would have never spilled my guts to you like I just did."

Kat returned his smile. "Spilling your guts can be quite healthy and we'll get the Utopia situation straightened out. I'll be in the office in the morning, so we can work on making a time and date log. It would be nice if we had that all together by Monday morning when we meet with Lloyd and Emily."

He squeezed her hand, then released it and took another sip of his coffee. "If we're going to start early in the morning, then I guess I should get out of here and let you get some sleep."

He made no effort to move and she knew he was waiting to see if an invitation upstairs was in the cards. How she wanted to take him up to her room, especially now that he still seemed oddly vulnerable.

"Nate." She leaned closer to him, breathing in the scent of him. She'd never wanted him more than she did at that moment. She knew she had to be strong. "Nate, we can't go back to what we had before. If we make love, then it will just be harder on both of us."

He nodded and stood, reluctance showing in his slow rise and his beautiful eyes. "Of course, you're right. I guess I should get home. I have a feeling we're going to have a long day tomorrow. You ready to go upstairs?"

"No, I'm going to sit here for a few minutes and finish my coffee," she said. "Go on, Nate. Go home and get a good night's sleep." He hesitated a minute, obviously reluctant to leave her alone in the bar. "I'll be fine," she assured him.

"Then I'll see you in the morning?"

She nodded and watched as he pulled on his coat, then left the bar. She finished the coffee in her cup, then gestured to the bartender for a refill.

She knew sleep was still far away and there was nothing she hated more than going to bed and tossing and turning. Her head was too filled with Nate to sleep, too full of the things he'd said and the things he hadn't said.

Was it any wonder he was a loner? Two antisocial eggheads who'd discouraged him from interacting with others had raised him. His childhood also explained his enormous drive to succeed, to finally win the approval and the love of his parents.

Finally, it explained what he wanted from the woman he married and reinforced the knowledge that she was absolutely, positively, the wrong woman for him.

Chapter Eight

Lloyd Winters was a handsome man. Tall, with a headful of short, silver hair and blue eyes that radiated intelligence. He was dressed impeccably in a tailored navy suit and a gray and navy tie.

In the five years that Nate had worked for him, he'd commanded not only great respect, but had also fostered a deep loyalty.

As Nate and Kat entered his office, they weren't the only ones in on the meeting. Four burgundy leather captain's chairs sat in front of Lloyd's massive mahogany desk. Emily and Jack Devon were already seated on the two outside chairs.

Nate didn't know Jack well. Jack was Senior Vice President of Business Development and Strategy and the two men's paths rarely crossed.

All Nate knew about Devon was that he was a

sharp businessman who was often in the society pages with some beautiful babe on his arm. He was a handsome man, with jet-black hair and gray eyes that revealed nothing of his thoughts or moods. He nodded as Nate and Kat entered the room.

Lloyd rose and motioned them into the chairs directly opposite his desk, between where Emily and Jack sat. "Good morning," Lloyd said. "Emily tells me you have an update for me this morning. I hope it's good news. In two weeks Utopia is supposed to be up and running."

"Actually," Nate began.

"Dad, Kat told me she thinks the source of the breach is internal," Emily said, interrupting what Nate had been about to say.

"Internal? What do you mean?" Lloyd looked at Kat. It was obvious he didn't want to hear from Nate.

As Kat explained their suspicions and what they had done to log time and dates of the entries into the program, Nate wondered when Kat had found the time to tell Emily that *she* thought it was internal, what *she* had done in an attempt to rectify the situation.

As Lloyd, Emily and Jack continued to question Kat, Nate wondered why in the hell he'd even come to the meeting. When Kat had told him she'd set up this meeting when she'd bumped into Emily in the hall, she hadn't mentioned that she'd also managed to take the credit for all the work that had been done.

A small part of him knew he was being a bit childish, but he was irked by the fact that Kat was controlling the meeting, a meeting that had been set up to discuss the problems with *his* program.

He supposed he shouldn't be too surprised. After all, her nickname was Tiger Tech, indicating strength and a certain level of ruthlessness. She hadn't built a successful business for herself by not possessing a certain amount of ruthless ambition.

"Nate, do you have those logs?" Kat asked, pulling him from his thoughts but not easing the growing irritation inside him.

Silently he pulled the copies of the logs from his folder and handed them to her. She handed one to each of them, then turned back to Nate. "You want to explain what you did?"

"No, go ahead. You're doing just fine." His words sounded clipped and cool, but no one seemed to notice, except Kat.

She held his gaze for a minute, a frown flashing over her face, then she turned to her audience and continued to outline what they had done and Nate continued to feel more and more isolated from his own project.

He directed his attention to Emily, who was staring at the log with an expression of alarm. He wondered what she was thinking.

Nate and Kat had managed to identify and specify each date and time that sections of the program were tampered with. They didn't log every time the program was accessed and there were no changes or copies made. The log consisted of seven dates and times, the last as recently as the past Friday.

"I understand you met with the tech team Friday night for drinks. I don't suppose anyone got drunk and confessed to dabbling in technological theft," Jack said wryly, focusing on Nate.

"No, unfortunately, and if you look at the log you can see that all the accesses into the program were done during normal business hours, so it could have been anyone who has a password," Nate explained.

"Or it could be somebody who simply had access to somebody's password," Emily said.

"I'd like to take a look at the personnel files of the tech team members." Kat leaned forward in her chair. "I already know that one member of the team is having some financial problems, another has just bought an expensive new sports car."

"Just let Carmella know what you need," Lloyd said.

Emily looked at her father. "I think, Dad, that we have to consider the possibility that it might be Todd."

Lloyd raised a silver eyebrow in surprise. "Todd? Why on earth would Todd want to do anything to hurt this company? Hell, he's family."

"He *was* family, Dad, but he isn't anymore." Emily got up from her chair and paced the small space in front of where Nate and Kat sat. "I can't be sure, but just looking at this log initially, I can see at least three instances where I know for certain that Todd was here, visiting. And I know on all of those dates he was in my office by himself and could have easily accessed the program with my password.''

Nate saw the flash of pain that darkened Lloyd's eyes, knew the kind of betrayal he'd feel if Todd was responsible. Nate was nursing the same kind of feeling of betrayal as he watched Kat interact with his bosses as if she alone was responsible for their discoveries and work.

''Or with mine,'' Lloyd said beneath his breath.

Nate wanted to leave the room. He had a feeling Lloyd and Emily needed to talk, knew that if it turned out that Todd Baxter was the one stealing the program and screwing things up, it would be difficult for both Emily and Lloyd.

''Why on earth would Todd do this?'' Lloyd asked.

''There's only one reason why somebody would copy as much of the program as has been copied, and that's for money,'' Jack said.

''And Todd is unemployed,'' Emily reminded her father.

''But, from what he told me, he's on the verge of being hired for a great job with some company,'' Lloyd said, still obviously having problems even considering his former son-in-law as a corporate thief.

''He's been on the verge of employment for the last three months,'' Emily said.

''What do we do now?'' Jack asked.

''I'd like to talk to my father alone,'' Emily said.

•

"Let us put our heads together and we'll get back to you with a course of action."

"I just need to know that we're on course with the Utopia program unveiling," Jack said.

"Assume that everything is on track," Lloyd said as he stood.

It was an obvious sign that the meeting was finished. Kat and Nate stood to leave. "Kathryn, we here at Wintersoft, Inc. can't thank you enough for what you've done," Lloyd said.

"Nate…"

Whatever Kat had been about to say was interrupted by a knock on the door. Carmella stuck her head in. "Mr. Winters, I'm sorry to interrupt, but the German clients you've been expecting are waiting for you."

Nate didn't wait for Kat. He strode along the hallway to the elevator that would take him down to his office floor. He heard Kat call his name once, but he kept going. He didn't feel like talking to her at the moment, afraid his anger had the best of him.

As he stepped into the elevator, he saw that Jack Devon had waylaid Kat in conversation. Good. He needed a few minutes alone to deal with his thoughts.

As the doors whooshed closed, Nate leaned against the back of the moving cubicle and drew a deep breath, trying to get his anger under control.

He'd thought they'd been working as partners, but she sure hadn't acted like a partner in there. She'd jumped at the opportunity to shine, to steal all the credit and be the hero. And she'd begun the process behind his back in a talk with Emily Winters.

The elevator door opened and Nate headed for his office. The irritation with Kat seethed in him, burned in the pit of his stomach like an ulcer.

When he reached his office, he paced in front of the window, where the early-morning sun streamed in with shafts of warmth. The warmth did nothing to ease the cold that clutched at his heart.

He knew she was ambitious. That had been the problem between them five years ago. Her ambition had screwed up any hope they'd had for a life together.

He turned as the door flew open and she came in. She closed the door behind her and looked at him for a long moment. "You're angry," she said.

"Don't be ridiculous," he snapped. "Why should I be angry? After all, I only worked years on this project for this company and in the space of a single meeting you managed to take credit for everything."

She gasped and moved away from the door, toward him. "I didn't take the credit for anything, Nate."

"Really?" He didn't move from the window, felt the tension that stiffened his back and ached in his shoulders. "Your little talk with Emily when you set up the meeting for this morning must have been quite compelling. She certainly seems to believe that, but for your work and intelligence, the entire program would be ruined."

"I know she made it sound that way, but that's not

what she meant and I certainly gave her no such impression when I asked for the meeting."

Nate turned back to face the window. Wild emotions swung through him, emotions that made him feel half-ill. "Of course, I really shouldn't be surprised."

"And just what's that supposed to mean?" she asked indignantly from behind him. He sensed her moving closer and he turned to face her once again. She stopped in her tracks, a mere two feet from where he stood.

"I should have realized how you got your nickname, Tiger Tech—by being aggressive and ruthlessly ambitious. That's what ruined everything—your ambition, your inability to compromise."

Somewhere in the back of his mind he knew he was spiraling out of control, overreacting to the entire situation, but he couldn't stop himself. For the first time in his life his emotions seemed to be in control rather than his intellect.

Kat stared at him in bewilderment. She'd never seen him so angry and the words he was saying to her made no sense. Granted, Lloyd and Emily seemed to have forgotten Nate's presence in the meeting, but Nate's reaction was way out of line with the situation.

He should know his value to the company and that Lloyd and Emily valued him as one of their brightest and most talented employees. He should know that they had stroked her because she was the outsider and probably within days would be gone.

He took two steps toward her and she'd never seen his piercing green eyes glitter so dangerously. ''Tell me the truth, Kat.''

He reached out and took her by the shoulders, his fingers pinching slightly into her skin. ''You didn't love me five years ago. You played with me, used me to entertain yourself while we went through the computer course. You found Nate the nerd vastly entertaining, but that's all it ever was for you, right?''

''That's not true.'' In that instant she realized they weren't talking about the meeting they had just left. They were talking about their past and the garbage that had been left behind in their hearts when it had all gone wrong.

The pain of that day when he'd gotten on a plane and flown out of her life radiated through her now. Their goodbye had been stiff, formal and they'd never really talked about their feelings.

''I did love you, Nate. I loved you like I'd never loved anyone before or since.''

And she loved him still. She'd thought if she didn't make love to him, if she didn't allow him to kiss her too much, touch her in that way, then she could keep her heart safe from him.

She'd been wrong. Despite the anger, the betrayal, the hurt that radiated from his eyes, she realized she loved him as deeply, as helplessly as she had all those years ago.

He snorted derisively and dropped his hands from her shoulders, as if he couldn't stand the simple act of touching her. "Sure, you loved me so much you weren't willing to give up anything. You weren't willing to make a single sacrifice."

"A single sacrifice?" She took a step toward him, an anger rising up in her to meet his. "You weren't asking me to make a single sacrifice, Nate. You were asking me to sacrifice everything. You wanted me to leave my home and leave my family."

"I didn't know about your mother. Had you told me, we could have worked that out. I would have helped you with her," he said, his voice still harsh, angry.

"You didn't want to hear about my mother." Kat felt a pressure in her chest and knew it was her heart breaking all over again. "You didn't want to hear about anything. You didn't want to know me, know my dreams. You were so busy spinning your own little idea of the future in your head, you didn't want to hear about anything that might destroy the vision you saw, a vision that had nothing to do with who I was, what was important to me."

They circled the sofa, like two wild animals seeking the weakness of an adversary. All the pain, all the bitterness, all the anger they hadn't vented at each other before now hung in the air between them, making the room seem smaller.

"That's not true."

"That is true," she shouted, tears blurring her vision. "You knew what you wanted from me, but you never understood what I needed. I needed my work."

She swiped her eyes, stood still and continued in a softer voice. "I watched my mother build her life around my father's life and when he left she had nothing to call her own. She didn't know how to be anything but his wife. I wasn't going to repeat her mistakes."

"You aren't your mother," he protested.

"And I can't be yours," she replied in a mere whisper. She saw the outrage on his features and hurriedly continued. "You want a wife who can create the kind of life for you and your children that you never had with your parents. You want a stay-at-home wife and mother wearing an apron and meeting you at the door every night. You want a wife who will devote her entire life to you, filling the void that your childhood left in you."

She drew a deep breath and raked her fingers through her hair, fighting back tears that still threatened to fall. "I'm not that woman, Nate. I wasn't five years ago and I'm not now. But don't accuse me of ruthless ambition just because I love my work as much as you love yours. You didn't ask me to make a little sacrifice five years ago. You asked me to sacrifice my soul."

She walked over to the closet and grabbed her coat, then turned to look at him. He stood at the windows once again, backlit by the sun, so it was difficult to see his features.

"I won't go back to California until this job is done. I won't renege on my contract with Lloyd and Emily." She pulled her coat on, needing to escape him and the hatred she felt emanating from him.

"We're going to have to work together to see this through no matter what our personal feelings are for each other. I'll take the rest of the day off, but I'll be back in the morning."

She didn't wait for him to reply, but instead ran out of the office and toward the elevator, needing not only to be out of his office, but out of the building.

The argument had stirred all the old feelings she'd thought she'd dealt with a long time ago...the pain, the heartache, and the bitter disappointment that he wanted more than she could ever give him.

The only difference was now she understood why he wanted what he wanted, the needs that drove him to want a future different from hers. She understood, but that didn't make it any easier.

And now her heart was once again wrapped around his, but he hated her, hated her for not being what he wanted, hated her for intruding back into his life, and hated her for being part of the solution to his problem with Utopia.

He hated her and she loved him and the duration of her stay here in Boston promised to be sheer torture.

Emily sat in her father's office, waiting for him to return from his last meeting of the day. They'd scarcely had an opportunity to talk since the meeting that morning with Kat and Nate.

The more Emily had thought about the dates and times of the access into Utopia, the more certain she was that Todd was responsible. It broke her heart and angered her at the same time.

Mostly it broke her heart for her father, who'd never allowed the divorce between Todd and Emily to lessen his relationship with Todd.

"Emily!" Lloyd entered his office and looked at his daughter in surprise. "Carmella didn't tell me you were in here." He walked over and kissed her on the forehead, something he rarely did while they were at work.

"I needed to talk to you, Dad. About Todd."

Lloyd's smile fell and he sat at his desk and leaned back, suddenly looking older than his sixty-two years. "Do you really think it's possible he's responsible?"

"I've spent the day doing a little checking on the backgrounds of our techs. Roger Barlow is driving a brand-new expensive sports car, but he lives with his mother, has no other expenses and makes a good salary. He can afford that new car."

"Nate and Kat mentioned one of the other techs having financial problems...Lily, wasn't it?"

Kat nodded. "But, Dad, if somebody is copying the program and selling portions of it to the competitors, they wouldn't be having financial problems, they'd be enjoying windfalls. Todd hasn't worked for months, but doesn't seem to be financially hurting at all.''

Lloyd rubbed a hand across his lower jaw, his silver brows pulled together in deep thought. ''I just don't want to believe that it's Todd,'' he finally said.

''I know, Dad, and neither do I, but the truth is these security breaches didn't start until Todd started hanging around here. He would know where I keep my passwords and I've left him alone in my office on at least three or four occasions.''

''I can think of two times for sure when I've left him alone in here,'' Lloyd admitted. ''Todd would also know how to access my files in order to get my passwords. I haven't changed anything from the time he worked here.'' He heaved a big sigh. ''So, what do we do now? Confront him?''

''I have a better idea.'' Quickly Emily outlined what she had in mind. ''I think this will show us definitely if Todd is responsible. If he isn't, then at least we've managed to eliminate him as a suspect.''

Lloyd was silent for a long moment, then he nodded his head. ''All right, get it set up for one day this week. I want this matter resolved as soon as possible.''

It was too late to set up anything that day. All Emily wanted to do was go home and get into a tub of hot, scented water.

Initially she'd been worried before the meeting, afraid that Nate and Kat would present evidence that the personnel files of the single executives in the company had been accessed. Then she would have to explain to her father the little matchmaking scheme she and Carmella had come up with.

Thankfully, that issue hadn't come up. But, from the moment Nate and Kat had handed her the log, she'd felt sick to her stomach, certain that the man she'd once been married to, the man her father still loved like a son, had betrayed them.

In the next couple of days, they would know the truth about Todd. She hoped she was wrong. She desperately hoped her suspicions about him proved false.

Chapter Nine

If Kat had no integrity, she'd be back on a plane to California instead of walking in the cold morning air from her hotel to the building that housed Wintersoft, Inc.

She'd much rather be on a plane headed home than going back into the lair of the dragon. But she did have integrity, despite what Nate might think of her, and she wouldn't quit until the job was completed, no matter how difficult things were between her and Nate.

And they would be difficult. She'd had no idea how much resentment and bitterness he'd harbored toward her until the day before when it had all spewed out of him.

She also hadn't realized the depth of her love for him and the power he still had to hurt her.

She entered the office building and headed for the elevator, her thoughts still consumed with Nate. She couldn't believe that he thought her underhanded enough to run to Emily and take credit for all the work that had been accomplished over the past two and a half weeks. And she still couldn't believe how much it hurt her to know that he had loved her and the price of his love had been too high.

She simply wasn't the kind of woman who could sacrifice everything she was, everything she hoped to be in the name of love. She didn't want a man to be her life. She wanted a man who would share her life.

"Watch out, he's spoiling for a fight," Nate's secretary, Mary, said as Kat passed her desk.

"No problem. I'm feeling a bit feisty myself today. I can handle him, but thanks for the heads-up." Kat drew a deep breath, opened the office door and stepped inside.

Nate sat at his desk in front of his computer monitor and didn't acknowledge her presence in any way. So that's the way it's going to be, she thought as she hung her coat in the closet, then walked over and sat in her chair.

"Good morning," she said, trying to inject as much cheerfulness as possible into her tone. Cranky people hated cheerful ones.

He grunted like a caveman and she wanted to box his ears. No matter what acrimony he felt toward her, he knew they had to work together. He could at least attempt a little civility.

"Have you heard from Emily this morning? Has she spoken to you about the next course of action?" she asked.

Nate glanced at her, his eyes holding a hard green glint. "Oh, I'm sure you'll probably hear something from her before I will. After all, you're the great Tiger Tech. I just work here."

"Funny, I don't remember that about you."

"Remember what?" His frown would have been positively daunting to most people.

"That you can be so incredibly infantile."

He snorted and looked back at his monitor. "Better childish than a backstabbing brownnoser," he muttered.

"I didn't backstab or brownnose anyone," she protested, an edge of anger causing her voice to rise half an octave. "You, on the other hand, probably need a diaper change because you're so full of—"

"Enough!" He slammed his palms down on top of the desk. "I am not going to spend the day trading insults with you."

"You started it," she replied, then wondered if it could be catching, because she sounded as childish as he had.

She saw on Nate's monitor that he wasn't working in the Utopia program, but instead was in a different program.

Unsure what she was supposed to do, she pulled up a game of Solitaire. As she played the game she couldn't help but think of the man seated next to her.

Five years ago she'd watched a transformation take place in him. He'd opened like a flower to the sun in the time they'd spent together. He'd gone from a driven, ambitious loner who hadn't taken time to play to a well-balanced man, still driven and ambitious, but also eager to embrace laughter and life.

She'd seen glimpses of that well-balanced man in the few weeks she'd been here. She'd also sensed a deep loneliness inside him, a loneliness she wished she could banish.

Sadness swept through her as she recognized that he'd become that lonely, isolated man once again. Only this time she also saw the bitterness that encased his heart where she was concerned.

"How many games of that do you intend to play?" he asked curtly when she'd begun her fifth game.

"I don't know. My record is a hundred and fifty-three games in a single day. Why? Am I bothering you?" She hoped so because he sure as heck was bothering her.

"I was just going to say that there's really no point in your being here. If you want to go back to your hotel, I'll call you when Emily lets me know what's next."

"That all right. I'm here now. I'll stay."

He grunted and returned his complete attention to the computer screen.

Kat played Solitaire until noon, then left Nate's office for lunch. She opted for the coffee shop in the lobby, preferring to eat alone than with a bunch of chatting friends. She didn't feel much like socializing.

Despite her facade of nonchalance in Nate's office, she was filled with a heartache that was huge. First, it hurt her that Nate truly believed she'd gone behind his back and claimed all the glory, made Emily think she'd done all the work. That he would even entertain the slightest belief that she was that kind of person hurt.

The coffee shop was elegant and hushed. Only a handful of diners were eating lunch and they all sat together at a large round table near the windows.

Kat sat in the plush chair at a smaller table and ordered the soup of the day and a freshly baked wheat roll from an impeccably groomed waitress.

As she waited for her order, she couldn't help it that her thoughts returned to Nate. He couldn't help who he was, just as she couldn't help who she was. Childhood experiences had shaped them into the people they had become.

She now understood the forces that drove him into wanting a stay-at-home June Cleaver kind of wife. She also understood the forces that drove her to need her work, something that was hers alone, something that made her proud and happy.

He'd spoken of sacrifices, but he'd never spoken of compromise. Five years ago it had been all or nothing with him and even if she told him she still loved him, would love to have a life with him, she had a feeling he would still want all or nothing.

For some reason, this pain of hopelessness where romance with Nate was concerned seemed deeper, harsher than it had five years ago.

She ate her lunch slowly, her eyes drifting often to the windows. Given enough time, she could have grown to love Boston, especially if it meant being with Nate.

But it was obvious from their conversation the day before that Nate no longer loved her, had never forgiven her and couldn't wait to see the tail end of her in transit back to California.

She was just about to leave when she nearly collided with Emily coming in. "Kat! Hi. I see you finally decided to check out the coffee shop instead of eating in the cafeteria."

"Yes, I needed a little quiet time and the one thing the cafeteria isn't, is quiet. If you don't mind, I'd like to speak with you for just a minute."

"Sure." Emily gestured to a nearby table. "Let's sit." The two women sat across from each other at the small table. "I always eat here because of the quiet," Emily said, then smiled. "This is the only place in the company to find a moment of peace."

Peace. That's what Kat was seeking and she knew she wouldn't have that until she made sure she'd rectified any illusion that she alone was responsible for the information they'd gathered about the hacker and the Utopia program.

"Emily, I just wanted to make sure that you and your father understood that Nate is a brilliant man, and I really had very little to do with the discovery that the source of the security breach of the Utopia program was internal.''

"Trust me, both my father and I realize how valuable Nate is to this company. What made you think we might think otherwise?''

Kat shifted uncomfortably on her chair. "At the meeting yesterday morning, I did all the talking and I was afraid that you and Mr. Winters might think that somehow meant I did all the work.'' Kat grinned. "I'm the mouthy one of the duo and I just wanted to make sure Nate got the credit he deserved.''

"That's very sweet of you, Kat,'' Emily replied. "And completely unnecessary. While my father and I appreciate what you've done to help Nate get on top of this problem quickly, both of us also know that Nate could have handled it alone had we had more time.''

Kat nodded, glad that Emily and her father appreciated Nate and understood that Kat wasn't solely responsible for what had been done so far. It was the only thing Kat knew to do to make sure that she did nothing more to hurt Nate.

She stood as the waitress approached Emily's table. "I'll just get out of here and let you eat your lunch in peace.''

"I'm working on something that I'm not yet ready to share with you and Nate. If everything works out all right, I should be set up to discuss it with you both first thing in the morning.''

Kat nodded. "Sounds good."

"I'm sure you're eager to get back to sunny California."

Kat shrugged. "Whenever, although I've certainly found Boston a charming town, what little I've seen of it."

"Make sure you take some time to visit the sights before you go home," Emily said.

"Will do," Kat said, then murmured a goodbye and left the coffee shop.

As she headed back to Nate's office she knew she'd do no such thing. Why take the time to fall in love with a city where you never intended to live? Why spend another day in the town that had produced the man you loved when there was no future here?

Nate realized now why his parents had never allowed emotions to be a part of their lives. Once you opened the door to your emotions, you felt everything more intensely.

Nate had never felt on edge like he had ever since his emotional confrontation with Kat the day before. He felt as if every nerve he possessed was exposed.

He couldn't help but be relieved when she'd left for lunch. He needed some space from her, an absence of her scent in the air, a break from her presence next to him.

The moment she left for lunch, he got up from his desk and walked over to the windows. It was snowing again, tiny flecks of crystal that sparkled and danced on their way down to earth.

Kat was like one of those snowflakes. Her individuality, her bright laughter, her very essence had danced and sparkled her way right into his heart.

The door to his office opened, then closed and he turned away from the window to see that she had returned. He blinked and looked at his watch, surprised to discover that he'd been standing at the window and staring out for nearly an hour.

"Why did you take this job?" he asked. "You knew I worked here. Why didn't you just turn down the offer when it was made?"

He didn't think his tone was accusing, but it must have been somewhat accusatory for her chin raised a notch as if preparing for a battle. "What was I supposed to do? Call and get your permission before taking the job?"

"I'm serious, Kat." He moved from the window to the sofa and sank down, feeling more tired than he had in years. "I'd really like to know why you came here."

She drew a deep sigh, raced a hand through her short hair and sat at the opposite end of the sofa from him. "I don't know, I was bored, ready for a new adventure and to be perfectly honest, I was curious."

"Curious?"

"About you." Her eyes at the moment picked up the hue from her navy sweater, making them appear more blue than hazel. "There have been times in the past five years that you've crossed my mind. I would wonder how you were doing, if you were happy, if you'd married. I decided to come out here and answer those questions for myself.''

He'd crossed her mind. He wished he could count the times she'd crossed his in the past five years. A hundred? A thousand? Ten thousand?

He stood, unable to help the bitterness that still ached inside him. ''So, now you know. I'm doing well. I'm happy and I'm not married. You could have called me on the phone and asked me those questions.''

''You're right,'' she said softly, and he thought he heard a touch of pain in her voice. ''In hindsight, my coming here was a mistake. It's stirred up a past that was better left alone and for that I'm sorry.''

For just a brief moment he thought he saw tears glistening in her eyes. It stunned him. In all the time they had spent together he had never seen her cry. She hadn't even cried on that last day when she'd stood in the airport and watched him board a plane to return to Boston.

He turned away, uncomfortable with her show of emotions, even more uncomfortable by the emotions sweeping through him. Work. It was the way he dealt with emotions, by losing himself in the technology of computer science.

He didn't look at her again. He sat down at his computer and pulled up the program he'd been working on. When she sat down and began a game of Solitaire, he didn't say a word.

Emily stood in her kitchen, waiting for the teakettle to announce hot water for tea and eyeing the cordless phone that sat on the counter. She'd spent the afternoon working with technical experts in a field she knew nothing about and had never considered using before.

It had been an education...and a necessity. And tomorrow, if all went the way it was supposed to they would know for sure if Todd was betraying them or was innocent. All she had to do was make the phone call that would set it up.

Waiting for the teakettle, she sat at her kitchen table, her thoughts consumed with the man she had married, the man she had then divorced.

When she'd married Todd, she'd had high hopes for their future together. She wasn't crazy, mad in love with him, but she liked him. He was smart and fun and he loved the company as much as she did. She hadn't recognized that beneath his pleasant, easy-going facade lay an extremely ambitious man, a man who intended to run the company and control Emily's life.

His ambition for taking over Wintersoft, Inc. after Emily's father's retirement had been thwarted by the divorce. It was the memory of that sharp ambition that occasionally burned in his pale blue eyes that made her wonder if he was capable of stealing from the company he'd once loved.

She jumped as the teakettle whistled, and poured the boiling water into a cup. She dunked a tea bag several times, then added a spoonful of sugar and carried both the cup of tea and the phone to the table.

She sat once again, eyeing the phone with dread. She took a sip of the hot tea, unsurprised to find that it did nothing to warm the chill that seemed to have taken possession of her since the moment she'd looked at the logs Nate and Kat had provided.

Nate and Kat. There was definitely something between the two of them, she mused.

They had looked at each other with a hunger, a simmering desire that had been palpable in the room. She'd certainly never felt that kind of passion for Todd or any other man.

Thoughts of Todd returned her to the present situation.

"Time to bite the bullet," she muttered as she picked up the phone. She punched in Todd's home phone number. She didn't have to wait long. He answered on the first ring. He'd never been able to stand a ringing telephone.

"Todd, it's me...Emily."

"Emily!" His deep voice radiated with pleasant surprise. "How nice to hear your voice."

"Am I catching you at a bad time?" she asked.

"No, not at all. I was just getting ready to go over some paperwork."

She wondered what kind of paperwork he'd have to go over? Something about the Utopia program perhaps? She forced her mind back to what she had to do. "Todd, I can't tell you how much I appreciated the trinket box you gave me last week. It looks so lovely with the others."

"I'm glad you like it." His voice was soft, smooth, almost caressing in nature. She remembered that tone from the days when he had been courting her. "I miss you, Emily."

His words shocked her but played right into her scheme. "I miss you, too, Todd." The words tasted bitter in her mouth. "Todd, why don't we have lunch together tomorrow? We can talk about…things."

"I can't think of anything I'd rather do," he replied.

"Why don't you come to my office. Meet me there about eleven," Emily suggested. "We can leave from there, go someplace nice and quiet."

"Sounds wonderful," Todd replied, then in that same gentle voice, he added, "I never got over you, Emily."

"We'll talk tomorrow," she said, unable to keep up the pretense any longer. "I'll see you at eleven in my office."

She breathed a sigh of relief as she hung up. And so the die was cast. Sipping her tea, a flutter of anticipation and dread mingled together and swept through her.

If Todd was the guilty party, they'd probably know

at noon tomorrow. If he wasn't the guilty party then they were back to square one, not knowing who was accessing the program and stealing it segment by segment.

She would also have to tell Todd that she had no intentions of renewing their relationship. He'd be angry at her ploy, her father would probably be mad at her and things would be worse than ever.

She hoped she wasn't making a mistake, but she had to follow her instincts. They were the same instincts that had once had her marry Todd…and that had been the biggest mistake of her life.

Chapter Ten

Kat and Nate had spent another silent morning when at ten-thirty Nate's secretary, Mary, stuck her head in the door. "Mr. Leeman, Mr. Winters would like to see you and Ms. Sanderson in his office right away."

Nate exchanged a glance with Kat. "Looks like we're about to learn the plan of action," he said.

She nodded and hoped he was right. She couldn't take another day of sitting next to Nate in silence, wanting to reach out to him but knowing there was no point.

All she wanted to do now was get this job finished and leave cold, snowy Boston behind. She only hoped the warmth of California and home would be able to banish the cold that had encased her heart since the day she and Nate had fought.

As they walked to Lloyd's office, she could smell

the scent of him, a scent that had become achingly familiar to her. Throughout the past two days it had frightened her just a little to realize she was contemplating a life without her work, a life with Nate as the wife he wanted.

There was a part of her that yearned to be the woman Nate wanted, that wanted to willingly give up all that she was, all that she could be, just to be able to share his life.

Although the idea seemed incredibly romantic, she knew that eventually she would grow frustrated and unhappy and in time she would blame Nate for taking away a part of her.

Better to love him and leave him than to love him and make both their lives miserable, she thought as they approached Carmella's desk.

"You can go on in. They're waiting for you," Carmella said.

Nate opened the door and together they entered Lloyd's office. The sight of a large television sitting in the center of Lloyd's desk captured their attention.

It wasn't a normal television but rather a closed-circuit camera and at the moment the picture on the screen showed the interior of Emily's office.

Emily and Lloyd were both there, as was Jack Devon and a man Kat had never seen before. He was a big man with a full beard and a small insignia on his shirt pocket that Kat couldn't read.

"Nate...Kat, please come in and close the door behind you," Emily said. She gestured to the man with the beard. "This is Randy Elliot from Elliot Securities. I'll let him explain briefly what he's set up."

"I've got a hidden camera in Ms. Winters's office," Randy said. His voice matched his body type—big, deep, and with a confidence that marked the slight swagger as he walked across the room and pointed at a control panel in front of the television screen. "From here I can point the camera, zoom in on a specific area and record the activities that take place in that room."

"I called Todd last night and invited him to go to lunch with me today," Emily explained. "He'll be here at eleven. I'm going to greet him in my office, then before we can leave for lunch Carmella is going to call me away. I'll leave Todd alone in there and we'll see what happens."

Kat exchanged glances with Nate. So, this was going to be a sort of sting operation. Lloyd had said nothing, his features stoic as he stood near the windows.

Kat's heart went out to the older man. How difficult it must be for him, to consider that a man he'd thought of as family might be betraying not only the company, but also Lloyd himself.

If Todd was the guilty party, then Kat's work here would be done and if she was lucky she'd be on an evening flight back to California.

She looked over at Nate, her heart aching as she thought of once again moving on with life without him. She would never again take any kind of job for

Wintersoft, nor would she ever return to Boston again. It might take a long time, but eventually she had to get Nate Leeman forever out of her heart.

Emily looked at her watch, then ran a hand down her sapphire-blue skirt. Kat thought her hand trembled slightly and knew she must be nervous. "I guess I'd better get into the office," she said.

She was just about to walk out the office door when Lloyd left his place at the windows and gave his daughter a quick hug. It was the first display of affection Kat had seen between father and daughter and it spoke of the intense emotions at work at the moment.

Only Nate, Jack and Randy seemed not to notice the tension that was thick in the air, making Kat wonder if the tension was merely a figment of her imagination or the anticipation of telling Nate goodbye once again.

Emily left the room and Lloyd returned to his place in front of the window, his back to the rest of them as if he preferred not to be a part of the proceedings.

Kat, Nate and Jack moved just behind Randy, who sat at Lloyd's desk in front of the control panel. They all watched as Emily entered her office, shot a quick glance in the direction of the camera, then sat at her desk.

"Now, we wait," Randy said. "If this guy entered anything on her computer when she leaves the room, I can zoom in on her computer screen and see exactly what he's doing." To illustrate his point, he moved a lever and the picture became a narrow angle focused completely on the computer monitor. He moved the lever again to return to a wide angle that showed the entire room.

Kat moved closer to Nate to give Jack a better view of the screen. With each minute that ticked by, Kat was aware that the time drew nearer when she would tell Nate goodbye.

Unless Todd Baxter wasn't guilty. Unless she had to remain for several more days to find the responsible party. She was so torn.

On the one hand she wanted, needed, to leave, get away from Nate, and on the other hand she wished she had a hundred more days to spend with him, a thousand more days…a lifetime of days.

She cast him a surreptitious glance and knew that several more days…several more weeks here would make no difference in her relationship with Nate. He was as closed off as she'd ever seen him, as he'd been on the day he'd left California.

His defenses were firmly in place and he was in a state where nothing and nobody could touch him, mentally or emotionally. He was lost to her and to any overture she might make, because she couldn't give him what he needed…what he wanted.

"Here we go, kids," Randy said. Nate, Kat and Jack gathered closer to the screen as Randy toggled a switch and sound from Emily's office became audible.

Todd, lean and lanky, was clad impeccably in a

brown suit that emphasized his thinning blond hair. His overcoat was slung over one arm as he greeted Emily with a hug. "I'm so glad you called last night," he said, and reached out to tuck a strand of her hair behind her ear.

Kat felt like a voyeur, watching a private moment between two people. Before things could get too embarrassing, they all heard the sound of a knock on Emily's door. Carmella stepped inside. "Emily, Matt in accounting needs to see you. I told him you had a lunch appointment but he insisted I try to catch you before you left. He says it's kind of an emergency."

"Oh, dear." Emily feigned an expression of dismay, looking first at Carmella, then at Todd.

"Go on, Em, take care of what you need to." Todd sat in the chair in front of her desk. "I can wait."

"Are you sure you don't mind? This might take a little while," Emily said.

Todd waved a hand dismissively. "Go on, get out of here. I've got nothing else on my schedule for the rest of the day."

"All right—I'll try to make it as fast as possible." With that, Emily left the office and closed the door behind her.

A moment later she slipped back into Lloyd's office, her stress showing plainly on her pretty features. She joined the others in front of the screen in time to see Todd stand and begin to move around the room. He whistled tunelessly and Kat felt everyone's tension rise as he ambled to Emily's desk chair and sat.

Emily gasped aloud as Todd withdrew a diskette from his pocket and slid it into her computer. Her gasp drew her father from his place at the window. He looked at the screen and his face blanched.

"Let me just switch eyes," Randy murmured, and suddenly they were looking over Todd's shoulder, directly onto Emily's computer screen.

With nimble fingers, Todd typed in a series of numbers and symbols. "My password," Emily said.

"And the Utopia program," Nate said as the mainframe of the program showed on the screen.

Emily reached for the phone, picked it up and hit a single button. "Meet me at my office immediately." She turned to the others. "I think we've seen enough. Let's all go have a little chat with Todd."

There was a hardness in her tone Kat had never heard before. But Kat didn't feel sorry for Todd. What he'd been doing was not only criminal but also immoral.

Kat and Nate followed the others out of Lloyd's office and Emily flung open the door to hers, surprising Todd, who stumbled up from her desk. "That didn't take long," he said. "Uh...I was just checking my e-mail." His fingers worked the keyboard and Kat knew he was quickly closing down the Utopia program. He leaned down and removed his diskette from the driver. He forced a bright smile. "What's this? A party?"

"More like a lynching," Emily said. "Oh, Todd, how could you?" Two security officers joined them.

Todd laughed, but his laughter sounded distinctly uncomfortable. "What do you mean? What's going on?"

"Don't pretend we're stupid, Todd. It's most unbecoming." Lloyd's voice was harsh. "I'd like to introduce you to Randy Elliot, head of Elliot Securities. He set up a couple of cameras in here and we all watched you enter Emily's password into the computer and access the Utopia files."

Todd's face flushed with color. "And I'll take the diskette you have in your pocket," Nate said. "Whatever you copied to it belongs to Wintersoft, Inc. and to me, and now it's going to be handed over to the police."

Todd's face was so red Kat wondered if perhaps he was on the verge of a heart attack, but it wasn't a moan of pain that left his lips, rather it was a curse of anger.

He dipped his fingers into his pocket, pulled out the diskette and threw it at Nate, who managed to catch it midair.

"It's all her fault." Todd pointed a finger of accusation at Emily. "If she'd just done things my way when we got married, none of this would have happened." He took a step toward Lloyd, his pale eyes blazing with anger.

The instant he stepped toward Lloyd, the security guards moved toward him. Lloyd waved them back.

"I was your son-in-law. When you retired, I had

planned on running this company. That was my dream, but your daughter ruined it all.''

"And that gives you the right to steal from us...from me? To sabotage Nate's work?" Lloyd stepped back from him, a look of disgust on his face. "Sooner or later I would have recognized that you weren't executive material, just as Emily discovered you weren't husband material."

Lloyd gestured to the guards. "Escort Mr. Baxter off the premises and see that he isn't allowed back on site again."

"It's Emily's fault," Todd shouted as the guards each grabbed him by an elbow. "If she hadn't been so damned frigid, so hell-bent on working instead of just being my wife, then everything would have been fine."

"A woman's only frigid if she's with the wrong man," Jack Devon said.

Kat shot a quick glance at Emily, whose face was bright red. Kat wished she were anyplace but here, watching what had once been a family tear apart once and for all.

In Todd's parting words she couldn't help but feel a peculiar twang in her heart. It sounded as if they had battled the same issues Kat and Nate had years ago. Why was it men didn't believe that women couldn't be capable of doing two things—working and being a loving, supportive wife?

"Well, I guess that's that," Emily said, her face losing the color of humiliation and returning to an expression of competent professionalism. "Randy, thank you so much for your help."

"No problem. It will just take me a few minutes to pack up and get out of your hair," Randy said.

Lloyd turned to Carmella, who stood in the doorway. "Carmella, could you call all the department heads and tell them I want everyone in the cafeteria in fifteen minutes."

"I'll be happy to," she said, and turned on her heels and went to her desk.

Lloyd faced Nate and Kat. "I'll see you two in the cafeteria. In the meantime there are some things I need to take care of." He turned and left Emily's office.

Nate and Kat left Emily's office in silence. "That was grim," Kat finally said as they entered Nate's office.

"Definitely uncomfortable," he agreed.

She felt his eyes on her as she went to the closet and got her purse, her coat and her briefcase. "What are you doing?" he asked.

"I figured I'd just leave from the cafeteria and get back to my room. It's early enough I can maybe get on a flight to California this evening." She didn't look at him. She couldn't. It hurt too badly, knowing this was goodbye yet again.

She ventured a quick glance at him, hoping to see what? Regret? Love? His features were stoic, showing nothing of his feelings. "I'm sure you'll be glad to get your office back to yourself," she added.

He nodded, a curt, single shake of his head. "I guess we'd better get down to the cafeteria," he said. His gaze didn't meet hers.

They left the office and within minutes were part of a crush of people all making their way to the same location. Kat lost Nate in the crowd and there was a small part of her that was glad.

There would be no real goodbye. She would sneak out during the cafeteria gathering and go. Her leaving would be just the way Nate liked things—neat and clean, without messy emotions getting in the way.

The cafeteria was packed, people chattering noisily, wondering about the reason for the impromptu meeting, enjoying the break from the normal day's routine.

Despite Kat's desire to remain in the back of the crowd where it would be easy to slip away, Emily spied her from the front of the room and motioned her to join her, her father and Nate.

Reluctantly she maneuvered through the crowd until she joined the other three. Nate stood on one side of Emily and Lloyd, Kat on the other.

Lloyd held a microphone in his hand and, after a moment or two of waiting, he greeted the group. "I'm sorry to drag you away from your work, but I have an announcement to make."

The crowd fell silent and Kat knew it was a matter of respect that Lloyd didn't have to fight for the attention of the people who worked for him.

"Most of you know that we are on the verge of unveiling a new beta software program that will revolutionize the industry, but what many of you might not know is that for the past six weeks somebody has been breaking into that program, copying and sabotaging files.''

The crowd buzzed and Lloyd raised a hand for silence. ''The good news is we've found the guilty party and we're on track for the release date in two weeks.''

Everyone cheered and Kat felt a swell in her heart, the feeling of being part of something bigger than herself, something that was good.

Again Lloyd motioned for silence. ''I'd like to thank Kathryn Sanderson, who flew in from California to help us with this problem.''

Kat felt a blush sweep over her face as the crowd once again cheered. She nodded and smiled, slightly uncomfortable with the attention. She was accustomed to working in her office. The only thanks she was used to receiving was a phone call and a check in the mail.

''And now I'd like to take this opportunity to give my special thanks to a man who is not only brilliant at what he does, but has shown his loyalty to this company again and again.'' Lloyd clapped Nate on the back. ''Nate Leeman has proved himself to be the kind of company man Wintersoft needs and I can't tell you how grateful I am that he's in our corner.''

As the crowd cheered for Nate, Kat stepped amid the throng of people and headed for the nearest exit. She wanted to leave now, with the shine of pride in

Nate's eyes, with his smile of accomplishment and recognition burned into her heart.

She had thought she'd be fine. She'd thought she couldn't wait to get away from Nate Leeman, but the minute she hit the cold air outside the building, tears blurred her vision.

Must be the cold, she thought, swiping at the moisture that threatened to run down her cheeks. In her heart she knew better. It wasn't the cold of Boston that brought tears to her eyes. It was the cold of her heart without Nate.

Watching the final drama between Todd and Emily had only confirmed what she had believed five years ago. If she'd agreed to give up her work and have the sum of her life be as Nate's wife, eventually resentment would have grown inside her, a resentment that would, in all probability, have led to a divorce.

She was glad she and Nate hadn't married years ago. That didn't stop her from grieving now. As she entered her hotel lobby and headed for the elevators a million "what ifs" swept through her head.

What if their childhoods had been different? Would that have changed the adults they had become, changed their expectations and needs of each other?

She punched the button for her floor, grateful she had the elevator to herself. She couldn't seem to halt the tears that seeped silently down her cheeks.

That particular "what if" was moot. She couldn't go back and change their childhoods. What if she'd married Nate? Was there a possibility that being his wife, bearing his children, would have been enough?

Warmth swept over her, momentarily banishing the chill of her heart as she thought of making love to Nate, getting pregnant by him and holding a child of theirs.

Inserting the key card into her room lock, she shoved that particular image from her mind. That ''what if'' was also moot.

In the three weeks she'd been in Boston, even though they'd come precariously close to making love on the sofa in his office, he'd never mentioned loving her.

She needed to call the airline and pack, but instead she walked into the bedroom and collapsed on the bed. She loved Nate. She loved his stoic silences as much as she loved the unexpected gift of his laughter. She loved his intelligence and his honor.

They could be so good together. With her he loosened up, took time to enjoy life, and became more balanced and mentally healthy.

When she was with him, he made her feel smart and funny. She felt his respect and basked in it. And when he kissed her, she thought she'd felt loved, but she'd obviously been mistaken.

She roused herself from the bed and picked up the phone. Enough, she commanded herself. Enough thinking...dreaming...wishing about Nate Leeman.

Within minutes she'd discovered that the earliest

flight she could catch back to California wasn't until noon the next day.

She moved to the bedroom window. She was stuck in Boston with a broken heart and it was snowing again.

Chapter Eleven

"Come in," Emily called when a knock fell on her office door. She smiled tiredly as Carmella entered the room and sank down at the chair in front of her desk.

"Are you okay?" Carmella asked, her dark eyes filled with concern.

Emily shrugged. "I guess. It's not every day you find out your ex-husband is a thieving jerk."

Carmella offered her a smile. "We already knew he was a jerk."

Emily laughed. "Yes, we did know that," she agreed. "I'm glad we found out who was responsible, but I know how much it hurt Dad to learn that Todd was responsible for the problems with Utopia."

"Your father is a strong man. He can handle it," Carmella replied. "And at least Kat and Nate didn't discover that we've been accessing personnel files for personal reasons.''

''True, but I have a feeling they discovered something else. I couldn't swear to it, but I've heard through the rumor mill that they spent a lot of time together after hours while they were working. I smell a romance.''

Carmella's smile was big enough to light up the entire building. ''If you're right, then I'm glad. Nate is a good man and he deserves to find a good woman.'' Her smile faded. ''And speaking of finding good women, dare we hope we only have one bachelor left on our list? What do you want to do about Jack Devon?''

''Nothing. It's time for us to stop our matchmaking scheme.'' Emily leaned back in her chair and drew a deep breath. ''Somehow, the events of today have made me feel stronger. If Dad tries to fix me up with anyone, I'm strong enough to tell him that he can't control me or my life, that if and when I decide to marry it will be on my terms, with a man I love. Besides, I'm sure Dad has learned his lesson after Todd.''

Carmella's dark eyes sparkled as a grin crossed her lips. ''I don't know, honey. Your father is as stubborn as you are at times and there's only one man he's treated like a son besides Todd.''

''Jack Devon,'' Emily said, and Carmella nodded. Emily shook her head. ''Trust me, Carmella, there's no way my father is going to get me to date that cynical, secretive playboy.'' A vision of Jack flashed in her mind. With his black hair, gray eyes and attractive features, there was no denying his physical appeal.

The incident with Todd had left a bad taste in her mouth. Maybe someday she'd be ready for a relationship with a special man, but at the moment that was the last thing she wanted in her life.

''Trust me, Carmella, in this particular area, I can be as stubborn as my father.''

Carmella's eyes twinkled with good humor. ''Just don't ask me to bet on either one of you, because I wouldn't have a clue as to who to put my money on.''

Emily laughed. ''Trust me, I'm in control of my own destiny and I have no desire to hook up with any man for a very long time.''

This time it was Carmella's turn to laugh. Her rich, deep laughter filled the room as she stood. ''Honey, when that lovebug bites, nobody is in control and you never know when that bug is going to jump up and bite you.''

Emily was still smiling as Carmella left her office. Leave it to Carmella to lighten things up. The lovebug, indeed.

As far as Emily was concerned, her experience with Todd Baxter had given her protection against any future lovebug bites. She'd been immunized against love and she didn't see anything or anyone who was going to change that fact.

* * *

The moment the meeting in the cafeteria broke up, Nate looked for Kat. She'd said she intended to leave from the cafeteria and go to her hotel, but he'd assumed she'd say goodbye before leaving. He'd apparently assumed wrong.

He returned to his office and sank into his desk chair. The silence struck him like a hammer over his head. The office was filled with an absence of energy…the absence of Kat. Apparently it would take a little while for him to adjust to having his office back to himself.

The past couple of days had been difficult ones for him. He'd played his fight with Kat over and over again in his mind.

No matter how often he thought about it, he came to the same conclusion. He owed her an apology. He didn't owe her an apology for what he'd said to her about their past relationship. But he should never have accused her of going behind his back and trying to steal all the credit, all the glory for their work.

Her nickname might be Tiger Tech, but he'd been wrong to throw that up in her face. Kat was many things. She was unfailingly good-natured, impulsive and freewheeling. She had habits he found both irritating and endearing. The one thing he knew with certainty was that she wasn't underhanded or a glory-seeker. He owed her an apology.

He jumped up out of his chair. It seemed vitally important that he see her now, tell her he was sorry and had acted like a jerk.

"Mary, I'm taking off the rest of the day. If anyone needs to reach me, I'm unreachable."

"Okay," Mary said, her features registering shock.

Nate pulled his coat on in the elevator, hoping he wasn't too late, that she hadn't managed to get a flight out of Boston immediately.

It was snowing again and he tried to shove from his mind the memory of Kat dancing in the snow and laughing as she lobbed snowballs at him.

He'd had a million memories of Kat in the summer, her hair shimmering in the California sun, her body sexy and tanned.

Now he had winter memories of her as well. She'd enchanted him in the summer, delighted him in the winter and he knew that if given a chance, she'd do the same to him in the spring and autumn.

He picked up his pace, half-running down the sidewalk toward her hotel. He'd apologize and tell her goodbye, then everything would be right and finished between them.

He reached the hotel and ran for the bank of elevators. His heart pounded like a jackhammer in his chest. He needed to see her one last time. He wanted to look into her beautiful eyes when he apologized and told her he'd acted like a total jerk.

He raced down the hallway to her room. He'd never known such a sense of urgency, of need. He knocked on her door, a rapid staccato of sound that echoed in the hall.

She opened the door and his heart filled with the

sight of her. She'd changed from her business suit to a beige terry-cloth robe that emphasized the ever-changing colors of her hazel eyes and the red highlights of her hair. Her face reflected her surprise at seeing him.

"I guess you aren't flying out anytime soon," he said, suddenly feeling awkward and hesitant.

"They couldn't get me on a flight until tomorrow. What are you doing here, Nate?"

"Could I come in? I need to clear something up before you go."

She hesitated and in her hesitation her eyes flashed with an emotion that looked remarkably like the same emotion that had darkened her eyes on the day so long ago when he'd been the one boarding a plane and leaving her behind. She opened the door wider to allow him in.

"Nice," he said, and walked over to the floral sofa and sat.

"What is it you need to clear up?" she asked. She belted her robe more tightly around her slender waist and leaned against the door.

"What time is your flight tomorrow?"

"Noon. What do you want, Nate?"

What did he want? He'd thought he knew when he'd left his office and raced here. Now his want had changed. "Will you come here and sit next to me?" He patted the sofa next to him.

She looked lovely, with her dewy eyes and her tousled hair, and he knew if she sat next to him he'd smell her scent, that delectable fragrance that had driven him half-wild for the past three weeks.

She hesitated a long moment, then shoved off from the door and walked over to the sofa. She sat on the very edge, as if poised for flight. "So, talk," she said.

"Kat, I owe you an apology," he began. He swiped a hand through his hair, finding it hard to sort out all the thoughts that flooded through his mind. *Apologize and get out of here,* a small voice whispered.

She looked at him curiously. "An apology for what?"

Emotion pressed tighter and tighter into his chest, making it more and more difficult for him to breathe. "For accusing you of trying to steal all the credit. I know you better than that, and I acted like a total and complete jerk."

"Yes, you did," she agreed, then smiled impishly. "Of course it's not the first time you've acted like a complete jerk."

An unexpected burst of laughter exploded from him, and in that laughter the heaviness of his chest left him and he realized the truth of why he'd had to see her, why he was here at this moment.

It had nothing to do with apologizing. It had everything to do with forever. "Kat, I love you." The words blurted out of him.

She blinked and suddenly her eyes filled with tears and she jumped up from the sofa. "Don't do this to me, Nate. We can't do this again. I can't go through this again.'' She turned her back to him, as if not wanting him to see her tears.

But he had seen them, and they filled him with tenderness and a desire to see that she never had a reason to cry again.

He got up from the sofa and walked over to where she stood with her back to him. He placed his hands on her shoulders. ''I can't go through it again, either,'' he said softly. ''It was hard enough to tell you goodbye five years ago. I just can't do it again.''

She walked away from him and turned to look at him. The tears he'd seen glimmering in her eyes now tracked slowly down her cheeks. ''Then why did you come here?'' There was an edge of anger in her voice. ''I sneaked out of that meeting so I wouldn't have to tell you goodbye, so I wouldn't have another memory of horrible pain and heartache.''

Despite the anger in her voice, her words buoyed him. She loved him. It was in her words and it shone from her eyes.

''You don't understand,'' he said, and took a step toward her. ''I didn't come here to say goodbye. I came here to tell you I love you, that I can't live without you, that I want you beside me as my wife for the rest of my life.''

It wasn't what he'd intended when he'd left his office, but he realized now it was what had been in his heart all along.

''That's nice, Nate.'' This time her voice held bitterness. ''And I love you, and I'd love to spend the rest of my life at your side as your wife. But we both know that I can never be what you want when it comes to wife material.''

''Maybe my wants have changed.'' Again he swiped his hand through his hair, feeling more nervous than he ever had in his life.

This was far more important than any computer program he'd ever worked on. This was far more important than anything he'd been involved in for his entire life.

She eyed him steadily, suspicion shining through her tears. ''What does that mean?''

''It means I've spent a lot of time thinking about what you said to me the day we had our fight. It means that finally I've crossed the threshold into full adulthood.''

He frowned, frustrated by the look of confusion on her face. ''I'm probably saying this all wrong,'' he said miserably. ''My communication skills aren't exactly up to par.''

''What do you mean, you've finally crossed into full adulthood?''

He took two more steps toward her and gathered her hands in his. ''What I mean is that I now realize I can't expect somebody to come along in my life and fill the void that was left by my parents' lack of parenting skills. I have to face the fact that I can't change my childhood. I can't ever get back what was lacking during that time of my life, and it's time I grew up and moved on.''

Her tears had stopped, but her hands were still cold and lifeless in his. "I was a fool five years ago to walk away from you," he continued. "I was a fool not to realize that your intelligence and work ethic is part of what I love about you, and to take that away from you would be a sin. This time I'm not a fool. I want you, Kat. I want you however I can have you, with whatever conditions come with you. I want you to be my wife. Tell me you love me, Kat. Tell me you'll marry me."

"Yes…and yes." She pulled her hands from his and launched herself into his arms. His lips found hers in a searing kiss that held every ounce of his passion, his love and his commitment for her.

She returned his kiss, emotion for emotion and he felt the press of tears burn in his eyes. Never in his life had he felt so right, so filled with life and promise, so complete as when she was in his arms.

When the kiss ended, she leaned her head against his chest, as if satisfied to remain forever in the circle of his arms.

"I'll quit Wintersoft if that's what you want," he said. "If you feel you need to stay in California near your mother, I'm sure I can find work at a software company out there."

She looked up at him, her eyes radiating shock. "You'd do that for me?"

The depth of his love for her flooded through him. "I'll do whatever it takes to keep you in my life."

Kat had never felt so loved in her life. She, more

than anyone, knew his love for his work at Wintersoft. She alone knew the ultimate sacrifice he'd just offered to make for her, a sacrifice she would never ask of him.

"You aren't quitting your job, Nate," she said softly. "I work from a home office so I can work anywhere, even here in Boston."

"What about your mother?" he asked.

"My mom is doing great. She has a wonderful, full life and, even though she'll miss me, she'll be fine if I'm not in California."

Kat held his gaze, loving the look that shone from his beautiful green eyes. It was the look of love. "I want to marry you, Nate, and I want to have your babies, but I also want to work. I can do it, Nate. I can be the wife you want, be a mother to our children and work part-time as well."

One of his dark eyebrows rose. "Work part-time?"

She smiled. "I can make compromises, too."

He pulled her tight against him once again. "I love you, Kat. I love your competence, your intelligence and your beauty, and if anyone can juggle a baby in one hand and a computer mouse in the other, I know it's you."

His smile was soft and his eyes blazed with emotion. "I might just be a computer nerd, but I'm a computer nerd who loves you more than anything else on this earth."

"You might be a computer nerd," she replied, and

placed a palm on the side of his handsome face. "But you're my computer nerd."

Her breath caught as his lips once again claimed hers in a fiery kiss. This sexy, brilliant, complicated, loving man held her future in his hands and she knew without a doubt it was going to be a wonderful, beautiful future filled with laughter and passion and love.

* * * * *

*Turn the page for a sneak preview of the
exciting conclusion to the*
MARRYING THE BOSS'S
DAUGHTER *series:*

ONE BACHELOR TO GO
by Nicole Burnham

on sale February 2004.
*Has the boss's daughter finally
met her match?*

Chapter One

"Emily! Join me in the ladies' room?"

Emily Winters frowned over her Monday morning coffee and stopped short beside the desk of Carmella Lopez, her father's longtime executive assistant. Without checking her watch, Emily knew fourteen Wintersoft employees were taking their seats in the conference room down the hall, putting away their PalmPilots and turning off their cell phones, ready to start her department's weekly sales strategy meeting.

"I only have a minute, Carmella." And Carmella, the one woman in the company who knew all the gossip—and everyone's secrets—rarely took a minute.

"It's important."

Emily glanced past Carmella to where her father, Lloyd Winters, the CEO of Wintersoft, sat at his desk.

From the sound of his voice, Emily guessed he was battling the same problem he'd faced all week. Emily dropped her voice so only Carmella could hear. "I take it this doesn't regard our distributor trouble?"

A look from Carmella told her all she needed to know. She'd rather it concerned the distributor.

"I thought we decided not to pursue this plan any longer?" Emily shot another quick look at her father to make sure his attention remained on his phone call, then focused on Carmella. "I know how badly he wants me to marry someone here at the company. Enough that he's willing to go behind my back to pester my own colleagues into asking me out on dates. But now that we've managed to set up all the eligible men—"

"Except Jack Devon."

"Except Jack Devon. I know." Emily resisted the urge to roll her eyes. Just mention of the man's name, let alone seeing him in the flesh each day at work, put her on the defensive, both professionally and emotionally. She and Carmella couldn't possibly find a match for him. Not only was he a league above everyone else in the company, having been named one of Boston's Fifty Hottest Bachelors by *Boston Magazine*, he kept his privacy fiercely guarded.

But since Jack would never ask her out—pressure from Lloyd Winters or not—she didn't have to worry about him. Just last month, she'd overheard Jack talking to her father about a dinner party Lloyd had thrown the night before. He had the audacity to refer to her—to her own father!—as a "spoiled rich girl."

Her father had laughed, rather than defending her to Jack, making it all the more evident how desperate he was to find her a husband. She wasn't about to risk her professional reputation trying to play matchmaker for Jack to prevent the off chance her father could convince him to ask out his spoiled, rich-girl daughter. Even if Jack was the most handsome man in the company. Even if one look from his steely gray eyes sent unwanted shivers of desire down her spine....

If you enjoyed what you just read,
then we've got an offer you can't resist!

Take 2 bestselling love stories FREE!
Plus get a FREE surprise gift!

SILHOUETTE *Romance*

COMING NEXT MONTH

#1706 ONE BACHELOR TO GO—Nicole Burnham
Marrying the Boss's Daughter
Emily Winters had successfully married off all of her dad's eligible executives except one: Jack Devon, the devilishly handsome VP of Global Strategy. A business trip was her chance to learn more about the man behind the mysterious demeanor. But after sharing close quarters—and a few passionate kisses—Emily was ready to marry Jack off…
to herself!

#1707 WYATT'S READY-MADE FAMILY—
Patricia Thayer
The Texas Brotherhood
When rodeo rider Wyatt Gentry came face-to-face with sassy single mom Maura Wells, she was holding a rifle on him! The startled, sexy cowboy soon convinced her to put down the gun and give him a job on her ranch. Now if he could only convince the love-wary beauty that he was the man who could teach her and her two kids how to trust again.…

#1708 FLIRTING WITH THE BOSS—Teresa Southwick
If Wishes Were…
Everybody should have money and power, right? But despite her birthday wish, all that Ashley Gallagher got was Max Bentley, her boss's heartbreaker of a grandson. She had to convince him to stay in town long enough to save the company. And love-smitten Ashley was more than ready to use any means necessary to see that Max stayed put!

#1709 SAVED BY THE BABY—Linda Goodnight
Julianna Reynolds would do anything to save her dying daughter—even ask Sheriff Tate McIntyre to father another child. Trouble was, she'd never told him about their *first* child! Shocked, Tate would only agree to her plan if Julianna became his wife. But could their new baby be the miracle they needed to save their daughter *and* their marriage of convenience?

SRCNM0104